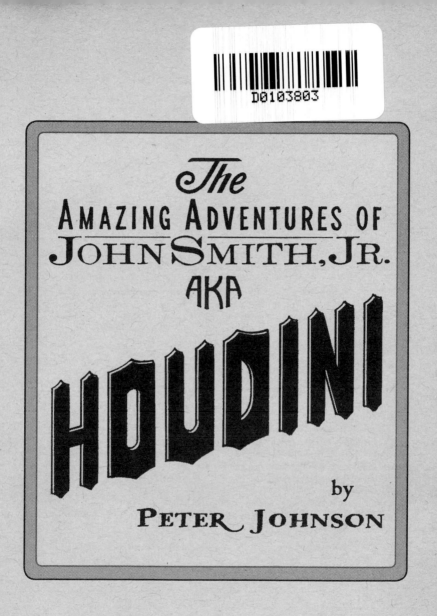

The Amazing Adventures of JohnSmith, Jr. AKA HOUDINI

by

PETER JOHNSON

HARPER
An Imprint of HarperCollinsPublishers

The Amazing Adventures of John Smith, Jr., aka Houdini
Copyright © 2012 by Peter Johnson
All rights reserved. Printed in the United States of America.
No part of this book may be used or reproduced in any manner whatsoever without
written permission except in the case of brief quotations embodied in critical articles
and reviews. For information address HarperCollins Children's Books, a division of
HarperCollins Publishers, 195 Broadway, New York, NY 10007.
www.harpercollinschildrens.com

Library of Congress Cataloging-in-Publication Data
Johnson, Peter, date.
    The amazing adventures of John Smith, Jr., aka Houdini / by Peter Johnson. — 1st ed.
    p. cm.
    Summary: Thirteen-year-old John "Houdini" Smith tries to write a book about what
is happening in his life, from his parents' worries about money and his brother in Iraq,
to his new understandings of people while he and his friends rake lawns in their East
Side Providence, Rhode Island, neighborhood.
    Includes bibliographical references.
    ISBN 978-0-06-198891-2 (pbk.)
    [1. Interpersonal relations—Fiction. 2. Moneymaking projects—Fiction.
3. Neighborliness—Fiction. 4. Family life—Rhode Island—Fiction. 5. Authorship—
Fiction. 6. Providence (R.I.)—Fiction.] I. Title.
PZ7.J6356Am 2012   2011019387
[Fic]—dc23   CIP
                                                                                           AC

Typography by Michelle Gengaro-Kokmen
14 15 16 17 18   OPM   10 9 8 7 6 5 4 3 2 1
❖
First paperback edition, 2014

For George Nicholson

ACKNOWLEDGMENTS

As always, a shout-out to Kurt and Lucas, who know the daily pains and pleasures of being a boy. Also, a special thanks to Phoebe Yeh, who pushed me to make a decent novel, hopefully a very special one.

MY NAME

My name is John Smith, Jr., but everyone calls me Houdini. If you can be patient, I'll explain the Houdini part, but first you should know what it's like to be named John Smith, Jr.

It sucks.

It's like calling your dog Fido, or your cat Mittens, like plain white bread dipped in skim milk, spaghetti without meatballs, or an old Ford Focus with roll-down windows and no CD player.

My father's name is John Smith, too. Well, really, it's John Smith, Sr. I guess we've had hundreds of years of this John Smith nonsense in our family, which would be fine if we were related to the guy who knew Pocahontas, but we're not. In the future, if some other John Smith decides to trace our family tree, he'll find a few other John Smiths hanging from one of its branches or stealing silverware from some rich guy's house.

But we *are* English, though none of us were born in

England. My father even has our coat of arms hanging in the living room next to a very ugly painting of an October sunset. He says hundreds of years ago someone in our family owned a castle with servants and hunting dogs, though I find that hard to believe.

All I'm really interested in is why my parents didn't call my brother John Smith, Jr., because he was born twelve years before me. His name is Franklin, and if you call him Frank or Frankie, he won't even respond. He was a big-time quarterback at my high school, and he played in college before joining the Marines. Now he's stationed in Iraq, fighting a war my father calls the "stupid nightmare of the most colossal goofballs of all time," meaning the politicians who voted for it. When he says this, my mother responds, "John, I've asked you not to use that word," but the "goofballs" (that's not really the word he uses) keep flying like spitballs.

It's weird, though, that my father hates a war my brother is fighting in. He's proud Franklin is a marine but says every time he gasses up the car he wants to strangle someone. By that he means Franklin is risking his life so rich guys who own oil wells in Iraq can get even richer. He's also mad about the economy, but then everyone in my neighborhood is afraid of losing their jobs.

WHY THEY CALL ME HOUDINI

First of all, I've read everything written on Harry Houdini. One day in study hall, I found a book in our library on magic tricks and magicians. The first page I opened to had a picture of Houdini, dressed in a pair of what looked like white Jockey shorts, hanging upside down and handcuffed in a Chinese Water Torture Cell. When I turned the book around, he seemed to be smiling while holding his breath underwater. I laughed because that's something my friend Lucky or I would've done, though Lucky would've drowned because he's the unluckiest person I know, which is why we call him Lucky.

That day in the library I became obsessed with Houdini. I read biographies on him and books he'd written on tricks and on other magicians. Most people think Houdini was crazy, but he was actually very smart and disciplined. "Genius is repetition," Houdini supposedly said.

What an amazing concept. When I first read it, I thought,

"Brilliant, now all I have to do is find something I like, then do it over and over until I'm great at it." Because Houdini meant that there were no secrets to his acts. He used to pretend he was a wizard because his audience needed to believe that, but, in fact, he'd practice a routine until he perfected it. And here's the cool part. After wearing himself out from all this practice, sometimes even he couldn't explain how he escaped. He'd just zone out, like he had tapped into some power from above.

I explained this to Lucky and to my other friend Jorge one day while we were shooting baskets. "It's like he had a religious experience where he could leave his body and watch himself escape."

Lucky laughed and said I sounded like an altar boy.

Jorge said he loved me like a brother but that I was a flake.

And that was the first day they called me Houdini.

HOUDINI WEENIE

Unfortunately, it didn't take long for some wise guy to add Weenie to Houdini, so sometimes I was called Houdini, other times Houdini Weenie, but at least no one ever called me Weenie, which would have been worse than John Smith, Jr. Well, *almost* no one, except for Angel Dimitri, who is one of the bad guys in this story, and so, like Lucky, has a name that doesn't fit him.

NO SWEARING OR SEX

In the beginning, I decided to write this book because I wanted to make money. We talk about money a lot at my house. We're always afraid my father will lose his job, and sometimes my parents argue if my mother buys something without asking him first.

Last week, a famous author came to class to discuss his book, which probably only three of us had read. His name was Mr. Peterson, a tall, skinny guy with a receding hairline and eyes as blue as Lucky's. Writers are always coming to my school. Our teachers email them, explaining how poor we are. *Dear Mr. Peterson,* I imagine them writing, *please find it in your heart to visit a few classes, since we feel you will motivate* (they always use this word) *so many of our students.* Then these writers show up, expecting to be lifted onto our shoulders and paraded through the halls.

We don't need their charity.

We don't want to be *MOTIVATED.*

We are sick of the word *MOTIVATED* or any word related to it, like *MOTIVATION* or in Jorge's case, *UNMOTIVATED*.

But we all want to make money, and Mr. Peterson said he'd been doing well with his books about "kids in crisis."

"What does he mean by that?" Jorge whispered to me, and Mrs. Guido cruised down the aisle and tapped him alongside his head with her big meaty hand.

Mr. Peterson's comment made me think about Lucky, Jorge, and me because we certainly had problems, and I figured if Mr. Peterson could write a book about this stuff, then it would be easy for me, since I'm one of the best writers in class.

Mr. Peterson said any of us could write a kid's book if we worked hard enough. He said we all have "authentic" voices, while he had to invent them.

"What's 'authentic' mean?" Jorge whispered too loud again, and Mrs. Guido made a return visit, shaking her head so violently I thought her wig would fall off.

I didn't know what "authentic" meant either, but I think Mr. Peterson's point was that, unlike him, we didn't have to pretend to be thirteen. And he was right. One reason I didn't like his book was because I couldn't believe the kid telling the story was really a kid. I knew it was Mr. Peterson pretending to be thirteen. It's like when I eat Kraft Macaroni & Cheese, and even though it tastes good, my mother's recipe blows it away. Now my mom, there's someone who makes "authentic" macaroni and cheese.

But Mr. Peterson did make me think about what it's like to be thirteen. He also made me want to write my own book because I know my life was more interesting than the kid he wrote about.

For one thing, the thirteen-year-old in Mr. Peterson's book never swears, and just about every thirteen-year-old swears, especially Jorge. We can't do it in front of our parents, even though our fathers swear all the time. My father says one curse word over and over, but Mr. Peterson said if I use it, no one will publish my book. He said kids' books with swear words "won't sell in the South or Midwest."

The South or Midwest might as well be Mars or Jupiter to me, since I'll probably never live more than five miles from home. But I think Mr. Peterson must know something because he got his book published, so there will be no swear words in my novel.

Instead, here's a list of words, and when they're spoken, imagine that the person using them is really swearing:

Goofball. (This should be my father's middle name because he says it so much.)

Take a hike.

Freaking. (Jorge has trouble completing a sentence without this word.)

Jackass.

Tick me off.

Heck.

Damn.

Privates.

No kidding. (This is my favorite.)

I realize that calling someone a freaking goofball isn't the same as calling them a you-know-what, but at least the sound of you-know-what will be ringing in your ears, and, hopefully, my own personal cash register will be ka-chinging when the kids in the South and Midwest buy this book.

Mr. Peterson also said a kid's book can't have "explicit sex."

No problem there.

None of us has had explicit sex.

None of us has had any sex.

Most of us feel weird just talking about sex.

After Mr. Peterson finished his lecture, Mrs. Guido invited us to meet him. Everyone was asking the usual questions, like if his characters were based on real people, or if he had kids. Then I blurted out, "If I write a book like you, can I make enough money to buy an Escalade and still have cash for college?"

Mr. Peterson laughed. "What's your name?"

"They call me Houdini."

"That's a good name. Houdini was an admirable fellow."

I had never heard anyone use the words *admirable* and *fellow* together.

"Do you think you have a story worth telling, Houdini?"

"I've got a lot of them," I said, though I was thinking mostly about what was happening to me, Lucky, and Jorge at the moment.

"Then we should talk. Maybe I can give you some pointers. One thing you'll learn is that if you write a novel, you'll learn a lot about yourself and never be the same person again."

"What do you mean?" I asked.

"Your characters change you. They get into your blood."

Because I hadn't started my novel, I didn't know what he meant, but all this got me thinking there must be other writers who could give advice, so I surfed the internet and looked them up. Sure enough, there were a lot of people who swore they knew how to write a bestselling novel, even though most of them hadn't done it themselves. They even made lists. So I read their ideas and decided to make my own list, which I'm calling "Ten Rules for Writing a Kid's Novel." I've already been following a few of them, but at the end of this book you can decide if I hit the jackpot. I guess if you make it to the last chapter, I did something right.

TEN RULES FOR WRITING A KID'S NOVEL

1. A kid's novel should have a lot of little stories that come together to make one big story. (One writer described it like "live overlapping electrical wires that make a huge spark." I liked that.)
2. A kid should be the main character. (Obviously.)
3. No swearing. (Got that one covered.)
4. No explicit sex. (Ditto.)
5. A few digressions will keep your reader off balance. (That's when you seem to change your topic but you really don't.)
6. You have to like your characters or the reader won't care about them. (How can I not like myself?)
7. Include a moral dilemma for your characters. (That won't be hard when it comes to dealing with Angel Dimitri or my brother deciding to go back to Iraq.)
8. Try to include a few lists in your novel. Kids like lists. (This one is a good start.)

9. Put in a few comic scenes. Kids like to laugh. (No kidding.)

10. Create a happy ending because people won't buy books that say the world is a lousy and confusing place. (Who can blame them?)

Although I like my list, I have to admit the ones I read made me think most writers are clueless about real life. One said, "Kids like books that remind them of their own nurturing families." Another wrote, "Kids today all own iPhones and Wiis, so you better put them in your novel."

Those two writers obviously never spent a day in my neighborhood.

But since you can't write just any junk, at least my list will give me something to follow, so if the smart kids in my school (who are usually girls) ever read my book, they won't think I'm a moron. Not that anyone in my school actually hangs around their lockers talking about books. Most of the time, we're all just trying to get by. That's what Lucky, Jorge, and I were doing that fall.

MY NEIGHBORHOOD

My neighborhood is on the East Side of Providence, but not where the rich families live. Instead, it lies between their neighborhood and the one people won't walk through after midnight unless they have a bodyguard.

Obviously, the kids in the rich neighborhood don't go to my school. They get shipped across town to a magnet school or they go to private schools. My mother says I should take the test for one of the Catholic schools that offer scholarships, but why should I get Bs at those schools when I can glide by and get As at mine? I also want to stay with Lucky and Jorge, who have a better chance of being astronauts than going to private schools.

Not because they're dumb.

Lucky is even smarter than me, smart enough to know he can't work for anyone. He plans to open his own landscaping business when he graduates, so why bother doing schoolwork?

"I'll study hard enough to get a diploma," he says. "People think you're a jackass if you don't have that, my friends." Lucky says "my friends" a lot, like he's a politician addressing the voters.

"The heck with people," Jorge said, "the goofballs tick me off," and then he went on a torrent of obscenities. That's just the way Jorge is. If Jorge were rich, he'd be seeing a shrink and on some kind of meds, but instead, people say he's "wired" or "crazy," depending on how they feel about him.

Jorge is short and thin and always wears a New York Yankees cap sideways. He dresses in baggy jeans that slide halfway down his rear end, and if you were to see him on the street, you'd label him a punk because he walks with an attitude. But he's really a good guy—and a great friend.

Still, you never know from day to day how he'll respond to something. Sometimes he's very mellow, soft-spoken, and would gladly volunteer to clean toilets at the old folks' home. Other days you'd think he had about fourteen cups of coffee. On those days, his left leg has a mind of its own, jiggling up and down as he clings to his desk, like he's afraid he might fly out the window if he lets go. That's when I wish his ear was an on-and-off switch, so I could lean over and shut him down.

It's hard to blame him, though, because there's always

something nutty happening at his house, partly because his mother has more boyfriends than Paris Hilton. A few have lived there for a while, others pop in and out. He's part Latino (that's his mother's background), but the identity of his father remains a mystery. My theory is that on the days Jorge's head is in fifth gear, he hasn't slept much. That's when his eyes are like slits, his eyelids puffy, like he got freaked by whatever demons visited him in his sleep. He doesn't say much about his mother, but then no one talks about problems at home.

Especially Lucky.

WHAT'S IN A NAME?

As long as I could remember, Lucky was unlucky.

One day a kid brought a nasty magazine to school and Lucky got caught looking at it.

Another time we were sledding down a hill by the rich kids' school and crashed into a fence. No one got hurt, except Lucky, who broke his ankle. Jorge said he should have sued someone, but Lucky said that would've made him a sissy. (But a rich sissy, Jorge added.)

And then there was the night when we decided to camp out in my backyard. We thought we'd be real Davy Crocketts and boil water from a local creek a bazillion people had probably peed in. We heated up the water on my grill, let it cool, then drank it, and while Jorge and I got the runs, Lucky had to spend two days in the hospital.

After that misfortune, as a joke, we started calling him Lucky, and it caught on.

But Lucky was probably most unlucky because his father

was a drunk. That wouldn't have been so bad, but he was a big, fat, mean, redheaded drunk who pushed him around and swore at him in public, especially when Lucky played sports. His mother, who was pretty nice, put up with his father even though he hardly worked, so he always seemed to be around causing problems. It wasn't unusual for Lucky to be looking over his shoulder, waiting for his father to drive by and give him a bad time.

Lucky *was* lucky, though, when it came to football. Like me, Lucky is big for his age and very strong, so local coaches had their eyes on us since Peewee football, especially me because of my brother. I stopped playing after sixth grade, but Lucky stayed with Pop Warner and was good enough to start in the oldest division. Although his team stunk, they won a lot of games because Lucky would run over everyone. His legs are incredibly strong and he constantly lifts weights. It's cool to watch his long, red hair flaming behind him when he shifts into high gear.

Girls like Lucky. They like his looks—the cinnamon-colored skin and small nose he inherited from his mother, and the red hair and freckles he got from his dad. Girls always go on about Lucky's smile, which is one of the reasons they don't flip out when he teases them. If the school ever votes on the coolest, best-looking eighth graders, Lucky and Fiona Rodriguez will win hands down.

But there won't be much about Fiona or any other girls in this story because if I start describing them I might say something sexual, and this book will never get published.

There won't be any football heroics either because Lucky quit the year after me, so now none of us play.

Why did Lucky quit? Partly, to tick off his father, but mostly because he had an idea.

"MY FRIENDS, I THINK WE HIT THE BIG TIME"

Leaves. That's how Lucky's idea started. If you want to be a landscaper, you're glad people hate to rake and bag leaves. Rich people hire fancy landscapers, but most people in my neighborhood ignore their leaves until the snow buries them.

Lucky realized this and also that the city wouldn't do anything about it unless someone forced them to. But we all know there's always money for what the city calls "community action programs" because they make politicians look good, so Lucky approached our local councilman, a guy named Mr. Gregory Gregory (no kidding) with a plan. He also tricked Gregory into notifying the newspaper, making him think our venture might help him become mayor some day. Lucky argued that if the city gave us the equipment we needed and ten dollars an hour, then on weekends we'd rake and bag leaves on certain blocks. No longer would they smell and decay, ending up as a litter box for every neighborhood cat and dog. He figured that if we did a good job focusing on only three blocks this year, then next fall we'd be able to hire more kids and we'd be the bosses.

Lucky called Gregory "oily" and said he'd probably been a worm in a previous life. He had thickly gelled, wavy, black hair and always wore a shiny, light-gray suit. He was constantly smiling and laughing and shaking people's hands when he'd show up to help old ladies unload their groceries or to rap with unemployed guys on street corners. All of this would've been excellent except you felt he wasn't paying much attention to those old ladies but, instead, looking to see if the cameras were rolling. He was a big dude who had played college football at some little school in Massachusetts, so when he was around, you had to take notice. He also called any group of two or more guys, "gentlemen," which ticked off Jorge for some reason.

Lucky not only knew how to work Gregory, but he also realized that if we kept our little business going and got the newspapers to write about it, he'd be in good shape when he graduated. He'd be, as he said, "the poor kid who cleaned up a pretty run-down neighborhood," and he'd end up with contracts from every rich do-gooder within ten miles.

"Hot damn," Jorge said.

So Mr. Gregory Gregory made it happen, and Lucky, Jorge, and I walked to Benny's Hardware and bought our weapons: rakes, edgers, clippers, goggles, plastic gloves, and even some thin masks, because in my neighborhood you never know what you might inhale from a pile of leaves. We decided there'd be no leaf blowers for us, not that the city would've sprung for them, anyway.

Our first day, we posed for a photographer in front of a brown two-family on Cross Street. Lucky stood between me and Jorge, his chin resting on the handle of his rake. I was told to lean into Lucky's left side and put my right arm around his shoulder while holding my rake in my left hand. Jorge was told to do the opposite, so we provided nice book-ends for Lucky. When the photographer was about to shoot, just as Lucky predicted, Gregory pulled up in his shiny black Maxima. The tinted window on the driver's side went down, and his big, happy, jack-o'-lantern face appeared. "Gentle-men," he said, getting out of the car and positioning himself behind Lucky. I could feel Jorge and Lucky squirming, but we all smiled as the photographer went about his business.

The next day, we ended up on the front page of the Metro section. The photo was in color, and because of our different racial backgrounds, we lit up the page.

"Freaking unbelievable," Jorge said.

"My friends," Lucky added, "I think we hit the big time."

"No kidding" was all I could say.

TEN CREATURES MR. GREGORY GREGORY COULD HAVE BEEN IN A PREVIOUS LIFE

1. A slug
2. A bloodsucker ("Ain't that the same as a politician?" Jorge said.)
3. A vampire from the planet Zeno
4. An assassin bug
5. The crack dealer's three-legged German shepherd ("That's one mean animal," Lucky said.)
6. The Incredible Shrinking Penis (A character Jorge made up.)
7. A big, black-headed python (We saw this at the zoo.)
8. The Headless Horseman (The only book Jorge had read from beginning to end.)
9. A toothless, blind warthog who was Angel Dimitri in his previous life
10. Mastodon poop

MY FAMILY

Even my father was impressed by the photo, though he said, "What's that goofball Gregory doing in the picture?"

"John," my mother warned.

"Well, it's not like he's going to be raking," my father complained.

He had bought a bunch of newspapers, and he and my mother had scissored out photos. She taped one to the refrigerator, and he folded another into his wallet. I told him the job would last only a month, until most of the leaves were gone, but he said he was proud of me, anyway. That was pretty huge for him because, like Franklin, he doesn't say much.

My dad's a big guy with curly brown hair and bright blue eyes barely visible because of his heavy eyelids, which make him look sad. He works the midnight shift for a cleaning company, buffing floors, so he sleeps during the day, then eats dinner with us, watches the news, insults politicians, and steps outside once in a while to have a smoke.

For work, he has to wear a blue cap stamped with the company's insignia and a striped shirt with his name tag ironed on. He says this outfit makes him feel like a robot, like the company owns him, and maybe that was why he was glad I was working for myself.

My parents said I could keep twenty dollars a week and that they'd put the rest in a special bank account. They wanted to teach me how to handle money, and that was fine with me. I knew how tough things were around the house and how difficult it was for them to save. My father works hard, and my mother has a job at a local dry cleaners owned by one of the meanest women on earth, who happens to be Angel Dimitri's mother. When my mother isn't slaving away at the cleaners, she's studying at the community college to be a legal secretary.

Besides taping a photo to the refrigerator, my mother sent one to Franklin, though we weren't too sure where he was. He was on an important mission, so he couldn't say much, not that he would've, anyway. Normally, he'd email or call us once a week, but every other week I got a special handwritten note, and when it arrived, I'd run my fingers over the letters, feeling the indentations the pen had made. The letter was always short. The first sentence read, "Staying alive here, Scout" (which is what he called me), and the last sentence was usually something like, "Study hard," or "Stay out of trouble," or "You really should play football."

Franklin didn't have to say much to make my day. I'm not embarrassed to say I love Franklin. We grew up sharing a big bedroom and when he left, something important went with him. His awards and trophies were still there, but, for me, sleeping alone was like being at Fenway on a night when the Red Sox were out of town.

Surprisingly, none of us talked much about Franklin, except at dinnertime when we'd say a prayer, or when some aunt or uncle or cousin would visit and ask about him. We didn't want to remind ourselves he was in Iraq and could get killed or have an arm or leg blown off. Every time I thought about him getting hurt, I couldn't breathe.

I knew my parents felt the same, especially my mother, because whenever the war came up or she'd see something about it on TV, she'd scurry around, rearranging dishes in the cupboards or she'd scrub the kitchen sink or bathroom floor. Sometimes, it hurt to watch her.

Also, every week she'd wash Franklin's sheets and make his bed as if he were still home. One day, when I was writing at my computer and she was working on Franklin's bed, my father appeared in the doorway, surprising me.

"By the time Franklin gets back," I joked, "he'll have the cleanest bed in Providence."

My mother sat down on the unmade bed. When I continued to kid her, my father glared at me, then joined her, placing his hand on her knee.

"He'll be okay," he said, kissing her on the cheek.

They looked like they wanted to be alone, so I went downstairs to get a snack because it was getting too "private" for me.

Still, it made me happy that my picture in the newspaper raised their spirits, and for a while, even at school, Lucky, Jorge, and I would be the focus of attention until the next fight broke out in the cafeteria or Sergio Frias's locker got raided for the tenth time. The only one who gave us a bad time about the picture was Angel Dimitri.

THE DIFFERENCE BETWEEN CRAZY AND MEAN

That fall, Angel Dimitri seemed angrier than usual, if that was possible. He's olive-skinned and has a three-inch-wide, two-inch-high Mohawk splitting the middle of his head, so that he looks like some biker villain from the future. If our enemies decide to bomb us back to prehistoric times, like my father says they will, Angel will be one of the survivors, straddling the neck of a *Tyrannosaurus rex* and swinging a spiked club.

He's also a big kid, a little fat, really, and he smells like fried fish. In gym class we sometimes have wrestling, and he's undefeated, mostly because when he works up a sweat his opponent has two choices: lose or be asphyxiated. If he ever slept over, especially on a hot night, I'd have to hose him down every fifteen minutes. Angel also has a weird mental problem. Lucky heard Mrs. Guido call it narcolepsy. Because of it, he sometimes dozes off in class and has trouble waking up unless someone explodes a cherry bomb in his ear. In a way, it's funny, but you have to feel sorry for someone, even a jerk like Angel, who has a problem like that.

Jorge doesn't share my sympathy. When he first heard the word *narcolepsy*, he said, "I told you, the dude does drugs."

"It doesn't have anything to do with drugs," Lucky said.

"Then why does the word have narco in it?"

Lucky had no answer to that.

Jorge also hated Angel's Mohawk, saying it made his head look like the reverse of a skunk. He often wished Angel would disappear, "But who'd want to kidnap a head case like Angel?" he said. "Isn't there some trick, Houdini, where we can put him in a wooden box, wave a white hankie over it, and he'll end up in freaking China?"

Surprisingly, before Lucky became friends with me and Jorge, he'd hung out with Angel because they grew up a few houses from each other. I met Lucky at the basketball courts when I was about eight, three years before we started to call him Lucky, and for a while, we all did things together until Angel started to pick fights with everyone. Then one day he and Lucky got into it when Angel undercut him on a layup. They started to wrestle on the concrete court, Angel eventually pinning him and almost tearing off his arm until I jumped him from behind.

Lucky couldn't shoot hoops for a week, so after that, Jorge and I decided to blackball Angel. Lucky said to let it slide, but there was something so wack about Angel's attack, it seemed better to avoid him.

Once, when Lucky and I were alone, he said, "Jorge can be crazy too, and he's still our friend."

"But Jorge's not mean," I said.

Lucky had to agree, though he always seemed to feel bad about the split until one day when we came across Angel wailing on some guy's butt with a Wiffle ball bat while two other losers held his arms. Then we heard Angel was hanging with a bunch of older punks, and that he was sneaking beer out his house, thinking it made him look like a tough guy.

"Real lame," Jorge said.

Still, Angel was tough, and I knew I'd have to knock him out if I fought him. He wasn't the kind of guy who'd give up, and I wasn't surprised when he hassled us about the picture, calling us a bunch of "sissies."

"Take a hike," Jorge said.

I just stood there.

"Don't you have anything to say, Weenie Boy?" Angel said. He was flanked by two skinny kids who got into so much trouble at a private school they ended up at ours. But I wasn't afraid of them because they didn't know how to fight.

"What's the matter, Weenie Boy," Angel said, "you too pooped from raking all those leaves?"

"Take a hike," I said.

"Are we talking about your mother again? You don't want to get her fired, do you?"

I wondered if Angel could really make that happen, so I started to leave when Lucky stepped in. "You know, Angel, some night you're going to be walking home, smiling and shoving a candy bar into your face and someone's going to smack you from behind with a two-by-four, and when they look for suspects, they'll have to interview the whole neighborhood."

Jorge started laughing.

"I'm not afraid of anyone," Angel said. Then he made an obscene gesture and walked away, followed by his two skinny friends.

Lucky turned to me. "Wow, that guy really hates your guts."

EVERY NOVEL NEEDS A VILLAIN

So why does Angel hate me?

Because he's jealous.

Try not to laugh when I say that. I'm no genius, I'm not rich, I'm not what you'd call good-looking, and I have no trophies on my desk. But I have a great family—by that I mean we're close—and I think Angel hates that. When he goes to the cleaners, he hears his mom yelling at everyone while mine does her job and is pleasant. She's also nice to him, even though he treats her like the hired help. I was at the cleaners one day when he came in for money and seemed confused by my mother's interest in his schoolwork and wrestling. When he ignored her, I felt like punching him, and I got even angrier when she gave him a piece a licorice she keeps in a bowl behind the counter. It was like watching her pet a dog that was about to bite her.

Sometimes my mother even defends Angel. "His family is having problems now," she once said.

"They seem to be doing okay to me."

"I'm not talking about money, John, and even if you have money, you can run into trouble." She was referring to Angel's father, who has a gambling problem and, like Lucky's dad, has a temper. "Maybe you and your friends should be nicer to Angel," she added. "Maybe he feels excluded."

Excluded? Boy, she didn't know our history with Angel, not to mention the lousy things he says about her. I couldn't wait until she quit that job, so I'd never have to hear Angel's mother yell at her, or watch her handling people's dirty clothes, while she suffocated every winter because Angel's mother wouldn't let anyone turn down the heat, even when it was a hundred degrees.

Angel was also jealous of my house. It's nothing fancy, but my father worked hard on it. It's nicely painted, and he laid down hardwood floors in the living room and bedrooms and built new cabinets in the kitchen. It was a project Franklin and I worked on, and after it was finished, we threw a party. My mother had just started at the cleaners, so she asked Angel's mother to stop by, not yet knowing how mean she could be. Unfortunately, she brought Angel, and they strolled around like they owned the place, Angel's mother sneering at our rebuilt kitchen, saying it would've been better to have a "professional" do it.

Angel himself didn't talk to anyone, and when my mother

took a picture of me, my father, and Franklin in front of our newly renovated fireplace, I saw him standing off to the side, scowling. The next day at school, he followed me around, pretending to snap photos, saying, "John Jr., sweetheart, stand over there with Daddy and smile." He probably would've kept it up all day if Lucky hadn't threatened to smack him.

For some reason, Angel especially hated hearing people praise Franklin, probably because no one in his family had ever done anything important. Franklin was a football star, class president, and now, to most people, a patriot.

None of this explains Angel Dimitri, though. To me, at least early that fall, the only good thing about him was that he helped me to get my novel started. Every novel needs a villain, and I didn't have to look far with Angel around. Unlike Lucky, I didn't care if he'd been normal when he was a little kid. All that mattered now was that he acted like someone had gotten inside his head and fiddled with a Ginsu knife. The only neighborhood person we feared more than Angel was a one-armed, black Vietnam veteran called Old Man Jackson, a guy who'll end up being important to this story.

"A BUNCH OF WIZARDS WITH THEIR BUTTS STUCK IN BOOKS"

Lucky was right about one thing: it was fun working for yourself. Even some of the neighborhood losers would high-five us when we showed up at their apartment buildings. But we couldn't choose where we worked. That was the deal Lucky cut with Mr. Gregory Gregory, who assigned us to three streets, not surprisingly ones where he owned property. Whatever house was on it had to be raked, unless the people who lived there gave us a bad time. Most of the old people who owned their homes got as excited as first graders when we arrived, knowing that for once, after October, they'd be able to see what little they had of front or back yards. But druggies and hungover people don't like the sound of rakes on Saturday mornings, so we had to be careful. One shady guy said he'd shoot us if we didn't finish by noon, probably because he was expecting customers. He was a big, fat guy who had a gray ponytail crawling down the back of his red velvet bathrobe. When he became agitated, his cheeks got so red he looked like a gangsta version of Santa Claus. Although we knew he was joking, we made sure to be out of there by twelve.

During our raking we discovered some very weird objects scattered around. We were prepared for cigarette butts, beer cans, and empty bottles of booze, even for the occasional shoe or pair of underwear (which made us always wear plastic gloves). But some things blew us away because they seemed so out of place.

Ten Weird Things We Found

A rabbit's foot

A dismembered Barbie doll

A dismembered Ken doll (found in a different yard than the Barbie doll)

A car's gas pedal

Two copies of Shakespeare's *Hamlet*

A golf driver

Handcuffs

A crucifix

A picture of a naked woman with her head clipped off

A George Foreman grill

As you can see, the whole history of a neighborhood can be found in a simple pile of leaves. The picture of the headless woman really spooked me, and I told Jorge that we should become "leaf detectives" and find out who she was.

Out of the three of us, Jorge was the least excited about raking, and spent most of his time whining. One day, he complained that he was working with a Houdini wannabe (me) "who couldn't even make a lousy pile of leaves disappear. That's the problem with hocus-pocus," he said. "A bunch of genies with their butts stuck in books, where they can't help anyone."

"He's got a point," Lucky said, laughing.

"Magic's not about tricks," I said. "It's about using your imagination." I have to admit I stole that from the internet.

"What the heck is that supposed to mean?" Jorge asked.

"I guess I'm saying magic is trusting in yourself." I stole that too, though I really believe it.

Jorge looked at me like I was speaking Russian. "If you keep talking like that," he said, "you're going to end up even weirder than Old Man Jackson."

Which at the time was a very scary thought, especially since we were about to come face-to-face with him.

OLD MAN JACKSON

To call Old Man Jackson's house a "house," you'd have to use the word loosely. It was more like a shack, about thirty feet long and twenty feet wide. Upstairs was a little room with a small window, which was always half open. I imagined Jackson sitting there in his rocker with a rifle on his lap, deciding whether to shoot us while we played basketball across the street.

Mr. Gregory Gregory had publically called Jackson's house an "eyesore," and he'd been on a mission to have it condemned and knocked down. He said he wanted to build a youth center there, but my father didn't believe him. Last year, after forcing a bunch of people out of a three-story house, Gregory bought it, had it leveled, and built a convenience store on its foundation. If this pattern kept up, pretty soon the neighborhood would turn into Gregory Gregory Manor, which really angered my father. He could handle oddballs, like Jackson, but he didn't like the way Gregory was intimidating people to leave, so he could buy up property. In Jackson's case, Gregory even called the cops a couple of times, falsely claiming there'd been complaints about Jackson's dog attacking people. Personally, the only weird thing I connected with Jackson's little house was the strong smell of incense creeping out its windows during the summer, but I never heard anyone complain about it.

Although Jackson's house was small, he had a huge front yard that was so dry and weed-infested it looked like a desert, and because it was surrounded by huge maple trees from neighboring houses, we couldn't ignore it. In fact, it looked like the wind had worked a deal with the trees to make Jackson's house its primary target.

The yard itself stretched from the house to the street and was enclosed by a waist-high, gateless, rusty wire fence, making it clear no one should leave or enter, and, in truth, I rarely saw Jackson outside his property.

"I think he's a vampire," Jorge once said. "At night, he turns into a bat and sucks the blood out of winos."

"Maybe his dog runs wild at night," Lucky said, "and brings him back scraps to eat."

The dog was a black pit bull called Da Nang, named after a battle Jackson had fought in. Periodically when you'd walk by, he'd sic Da Nang on you, and just before the dog reached the fence, he'd trigger a remote control programmed to the dog's collar, which would make Da Nang halt, then stare you down. It was frightening, not only because Da Nang was a pit bull but because he had one creepy, grayish glass eye. It was even scarier because Jackson would break into this insane, high-pitched laugh as the dog charged you, getting a rush from the look on your face. Jackson could be a real goofball, but my father said he had saved some soldiers in Vietnam and had received a Purple Heart, and that the government had cheated him out of benefits.

I had never really seen Jackson up close until we showed up with our rakes and paper leaf bags in hand.

It was a sunny, late October afternoon, and we had decided to finish at his house, hoping it might burn down before we arrived.

"I don't think this is a good idea," I told Lucky.

"A freaking understatement," Jorge said.

"Gregory said he squared it with Jackson," Lucky said, "so relax."

"Jackson hates Gregory," Jorge said. "I just don't want Da Nang taking my privates as a souvenir."

We probably would've spent the whole afternoon arguing, except Jackson materialized on his front porch, sock- and shoeless, Da Nang standing next to him at attention. Jackson wore old, blue overalls and a perfectly clean, white T-shirt. He was bald but had an untrimmed, bushy, gray beard. As he approached, with Da Nang walking like a trained poodle at his side, I noticed his one good arm was covered with tattoos. The stump of his other arm even had one. He smiled, showing a mouthful of different colored teeth, some missing, and he smelled like incense. "What's the problem here, boys?" he asked politely.

"Didn't Mr. Gregory call you?" Lucky said.

"You mean the black man who wants to be a white man?" Lucky didn't know what to say.

"Yeah, he called," Jackson said. "So you're the do-gooders I saw in the paper. Does that mean me and Da Nang have to make you cookies?" He let out this hyena-like laugh that made Da Nang howl.

"Damn," Jorge said.

"Watch your mouth, boy," Jackson said. "Da Nang don't like swear words." Then he laughed. "I'm just havin' fun with you boys. Hop the fence and me and Da Nang will go inside."

And that's what we were about to do when Angel Dimitri turned the corner. He was sucking on a lime Popsicle, grinning like a chimpanzee. Old Man Jackson hissed when he saw him, and Da Nang started to growl, probably sensing evil, like animals are supposed to.

Angel just laughed.

"I'm watching you, fatso," Jackson said. "I know it was

you who shot those apples at my house."

Jackson was right on that score. Two weeks earlier at the basketball courts, Angel made a catapult out of a four-foot plank and a large rock. Right before sunset, he placed a rotten apple on one end of the board, dropping a boulder on the other end, which made the apple hurl through the air toward Jackson's house. The apple came up short, but he kept practicing until one hit Jackson's roof. Then he made three more catapults and got some losers to help him, so he could fire four apples at the same time. That's when Lucky, Jorge, and I left, but I heard Jackson was almost knocked unconscious when he stormed out of the house, yelling. I could still see the leftovers of Angel's attack scattered around the yard.

"I don't know what you're talking about," Angel said, continuing to smile, his Mohawk twitching like a giant centipede.

Old Man Jackson made his thumb and forefinger into a gun and pulled an invisible trigger. "I'm going to get you," he said, "and when I do, I'll let Da Nang lick up the scraps." He walked back to the house, then turned to shoot his imaginary gun.

"No," Angel mumbled, "I'm going to get *you*, and I'll have something special for your dog."

Jackson couldn't hear him, but right before closing his door, he surprised me, turning his gaze my way and saying,

"The paper said you're Franklin's brother."

"Yes, sir," I said, wondering where the "sir" came from.

"Is he still alive?"

"Yeah."

"Good," Jackson replied. He stared at his stump. "They ought to shoot those politicians for sending boys to war." Then he disappeared into the house with Da Nang.

Angel took a long suck on his Popsicle. "Have fun, sissy boys," he said, walking away, followed by Jorge's rapid-fire obscenities.

"Save your energy for raking," Lucky told Jorge, and he was right because when we hopped the fence, we were ankle-deep in leaves.

GEARS OF WAR

I wasn't lying when I said Franklin was doing okay. But what I didn't say was that having a brother in Iraq sucks worse than being named John Smith, Jr.

At first, I thought it would be neat, especially after Franklin came home from basic training, jacked up and dressed in fatigues. Under his arm he carried a large, framed picture of himself in his blue dress uniform and white military hat. My mother set it up on top of the TV, and when he wasn't around, I used to try on his hat and jacket. I'd also stare at the picture—his square jaw and steely blue eyes—imagining him surveying bombed-out Iraqi buildings, while steadying his automatic rifle or crisscrossing streets, dodging bullets. I could feel his heavy breathing, wondering whether the next bullet or car bomb was meant for him.

But all our pride began to fade after he left for more training. What we feared most was Franklin being Franklin. We knew if he got killed, it would happen because he tried to save someone, or because he reached down to give a little Iraqi boy a candy bar while that boy's father, who was an enemy soldier, leaped from a closet and shot him in the head. My mother wished the Marines had trained him to be a cook or journalist. "They have jobs like that in the Marines, don't they?" she asked my father, who replied, "How the heck do I know?" He didn't mean to be nasty. He just didn't like talking about the war, unless he was yelling at the TV. He was also uptight because two coworkers had been laid off, and every morning I had seen him scanning the want ads.

So it's not surprising that during Franklin's final visit before being shipped out, he and my father tiptoed around each other. I'm not saying they didn't talk, but their conversation was mostly about sports, and Franklin seemed to be distant and edgy, like he was either itching to go to Iraq or worried about it. Sometimes he would sit in front of a bowl of cereal for five minutes before taking a bite.

One day my father was ranting about Manny Ramírez, saying he was a "cancer," and that the Red Sox were lucky they got rid of him.

"It's all about money," Franklin said.

My father was reading the sports section at the breakfast table, and Franklin was having a cup of coffee.

"I wouldn't pay to see any of those guys play," my father said. "They're making millions to hit a lousy baseball while the rest of us can't afford a hot dog at Fenway. It's insulting."

Franklin nodded, saying it made more sense to go to a PawSox game, the AAA team that played a few miles away.

And this was how breakfast usually went, with them going back and forth about batting statistics or how steroids ruined the game while all I wanted to know was when Franklin was leaving. Maybe my father felt that if he didn't mention the inevitable, it might not happen.

My mother just avoided conversation. All she did was cook. Anything Franklin ever liked would mysteriously appear on the dinner table. He especially loved peanut butter cookies, so after he left, we had enough peanut butter cookies to feed half of Providence.

What was nice about his last visit was that he paid more attention to me. When he was in high school, he was always busy with sports and school, and I hardly saw him while he was at college. But now we went to movies, played video games, shot baskets, and took walks around the neighborhood, talking to everyone we bumped into, like he was afraid he might not get another chance.

The only video game he wouldn't play was *Gears of War.* I asked if he thought real war would be like the video game, and he said, "No, real people die in real war." When he said this, I noticed my father standing in the doorway looking at us, his face gray and somber. He himself hadn't been in the service, but his favorite uncle was killed in Vietnam. Sometimes I felt my father had some secret knowledge about Franklin's future, and it scared me.

But it was nice to have Franklin back in the room, and I tried to convince myself he'd be there forever. Of course that was stupid, and one day he was gone, leaving behind a brand-new football autographed by Tom Brady. I don't know how he made that happen, but it meant more to me than if he had been really dramatic, which would've just made my mother cry.

TEN THINGS I MISS ABOUT FRANKLIN THAT ARE REALLY ONE THING

Franklin deciding to chill with me on a Saturday
    morning,
Then making me chocolate-chip waffles,
Which we eat in the living room while watching
    SportsCenter,
And bet on whether the Red Sox bull pen blew
    another save,
Then getting into my father's old Taurus station
    wagon,
And going to play miniature golf,
Knowing I can beat him in miniature golf,
But letting him win anyway,
So he'll buy me an extra-large blueberry slush at the
    concession stand,
Then going home and listening to him joke with my
    father about how he was behind but won the last
    five holes.
Franklin never seemed to get it that I always let him

win those holes, but it was worth it to see him happy. I truly believe Franklin could've been anything. He was one of those guys who everyone noticed when he came into a room, not just because of his smile and his size—he was at least six feet five—but because of the way he moved, like he was completely cool with himself.

Unlike me, Franklin wasn't a big talker. I tend to babble, and when I get that way, he puts a hand on my shoulder, or waits me out before giving advice. He's also big on community service, like handing out clothes to the homeless or working in soup kitchens, and his favorite phrase is "To whom much is given, much is expected." It was something he read somewhere, and at first I didn't get it because from what I could see, we hadn't been given very much. Then one day Franklin explained that we were healthy and loved each other, which was more than most people could say, so we had an obligation to give back.

But don't get the idea Franklin was a wimp. In my neighborhood, you can't make it past first grade without someone trying to beat on you, and there are always gangsta wannabes starting trouble. But no one ever messed with Franklin. Although I'd never seen him beat up anyone, I had watched him stare down a few guys, making them have to decide if a fight was worth it.

They always backed down.

BEING A WRITER AIN'T EASY

After Franklin left, I worked hard on my book, hoping I'd forget how lonely I was. Every night I tried to write for at least an hour. My problem was that I didn't know how to organize things that were happening to me. And my list wasn't helping.

All I seemed to be doing was taking notes on how people dressed or what they said, not knowing how to make a story out of it. I noticed how my father combed his hair, how Lucky had a habit of rubbing his chin when he was angry, how Jorge got especially wired at certain times of the day (like he had an alarm clock planted inside his head), and how Fiona Rodriguez would pretend to ignore Lucky when she passed him in the hallway, then turn quickly to see if he was checking her out.

It was pretty confusing being bombarded by all these details, as if each one of them was important. I even found myself focusing on people I didn't like—Angel, for instance.

I noticed he often looked depressed sitting at his desk, staring out the window at cars traveling down Hope Street. It almost made me think he was human.

The more closely I looked at people, the more I felt I could see into their heads. Although all this thinking wasn't getting my novel written, it did remind me of what Mr. Peterson said about how writing changes the way you look at the world.

"Very freaking weird," Jorge would have said.

A MOUNTAIN OF LEAVES

I've probably made you believe that raking leaves was always fun. It certainly was cool to find a lot of strange things, meet a lot of strange people, and be paid to hang around with each other, not to mention being photographed for the newspaper. But there was a downside, like raking leaves in the rain, or wearing plastic gloves and white cotton masks on warm, windy days. The masks protected us from dust and other disgusting airborne garbage, but also made us inhale our own stale breath, so that we felt like we were kissing ourselves.

Because of this nonsense, we decided to treat ourselves. Next to the basketball courts across the street from Old Man Jackson's house was a small field teeming with leaves. Every Saturday afternoon, after we finished for the day, we'd go there and rake for an hour. The idea was to create a mountain of leaves we could leap into. We made the mountain next to an old shed, which would be our diving board. On our last day, we agreed to order a few pizzas, organize a jumping contest, then bag the remaining leaves and return to our abnormal lives.

Other kids heard about the contest and planned to show up. Even Angel thought it would be cool, though, periodically, he came by with his friends to hassle us. "Why don't you grab a rake and do something?" Lucky said.

"Why don't you kiss your mother?" Angel said, which I guess was an insult.

Lucky didn't respond, but Jorge freaked out and called Angel "Sleepy," referring to Angel's constant nodding off and also to one of the Seven Dwarfs. It wasn't like Jorge to poke fun of people with strange diseases, but when you went up against Angel, you had to play dirty. That day was weird because Angel was walking around with a large plastic Baggie containing a big piece of uncooked meat soaking in its own juices.

"What's that for, you goofball?" Jorge asked.

Angel didn't answer. He said he would talk only to Lucky.

Lucky shook his head. "Okay, Angel, I'll play. What's the piece of meat for?"

"It's a surprise for your mother," he said, and his two friends laughed.

Jorge made a move toward Angel, but I held him back.

"Whatever, Angel," Lucky said. "Just remember what I said about walking the streets at night."

Angel laughed. "Don't worry, Lucky, or you too, Mr. Weenie, because I got a little surprise for all of you." Then he crossed the street toward Old Man Jackson's house, stopping by the fence. His friends blocked our view while Angel did something behind them. After that, they ran off, laughing and shooting us the finger.

"What was that about?" Jorge asked.

"He's just crazy," Lucky said.

"TAKE A HIKE"

We didn't have to wait longer than twenty-four hours to discover what Angel had done. Sunday afternoon I heard sirens, which isn't strange in my neighborhood because we're close to a hospital and because it's not unheard of for someone to start a fight.

After Mass, I got a call from Lucky, who told me to meet him at Jackson's but not to call Jorge. When I arrived, a white van was pulling away, and an ambulance and a cop car were parked in front. Jackson was on his porch, screaming to get into the van, while two ambulance guys stood around, laughing. A cop tried to restrain Jackson, but he bolted, hopping his old, rusty fence and chasing down the van, his stumpy arm waving in the air like a broken chicken wing. The van finally stopped and let him in. That's when we asked the attendants what had happened.

One short, redheaded guy with skin the color of paste explained that Da Nang almost stopped breathing, so Jackson had called an ambulance.

"What's so funny about that?" Lucky asked.

"It's a stupid dog," the attendant said. "So we just phoned the animal control people."

"What happened to the dog?" I asked.

"How am I supposed to know?" the guy said. "It looked like he was poisoned, but I'm not trained to give mouth-to-mouth to pit bulls." He and his partner broke into laughter.

Lucky shook his head. "First," he said, "the dog you don't care about has a name. It's Da Nang. Secondly, you're giving guys with red hair a bad name."

The attendant didn't know how to respond, so he said what guys usually say when they don't know what to say, which is "Take a hike." Then he and his buddy drove away.

As you've no doubt guessed, Angel's piece of meat caused Da Nang's trip in the white van. Angel wouldn't have thought of anything fancy. He probably soaked a cheap slab of steak in antifreeze and figured the dog would gobble it up on his next trip to take a dump.

"What a goofball," Lucky said.

"No kidding," I said.

It's not like we were crazy about Da Nang, but we'd never seen him actually hurt anyone. He just followed Jackson's orders. For all we knew, Da Nang might've been as peaceful and playful as a puppy when he was in the house. Whatever.

We agreed that Angel had gone too far, and that we had to tell someone, though we had no real evidence.

"We have to let Jorge in on this," I said.

"What are you, nuts?" Lucky said. "He'll just get out of control."

"Then what should we do?"

"I think we have to see if the dog dies, then ask Jackson what happened."

"You mean go into the yard again?"

"You have a better idea, Houdini? Got any magic tricks up your sleeve?"

TWO HOUDINIS

Lucky was right about my obsession with magic and illusion, but he didn't know the other things I had in common with Harry Houdini. We both have motion sickness, and we've both escaped injury a number of times, as you'll see later. Also, we're both superstitious about Friday the 13th. Whenever that day arrives, I pretend to be sick, so I don't have to go to school. I don't know where that comes from because I've never seen those Friday the 13th movies. The title alone scares me.

What we have most in common, though, is a desire to do the right thing, though I probably got part of that from Franklin. A lot of people think Houdini spent his life trying to trick people. Some famous circus guy named P. T. Barnum said that American people want to be humbugged, which means that they want to be fooled. But Houdini said, "In my own particular work I find there is so much that is marvelous and wonderful that can be accomplished by perfectly natural means that I have no need to humbug the public." He even spent time trying to debunk phony mystics who would trick sad and lonely people into believing they could speak to their dead relatives. He would disguise himself and come to séances, then, at the last minute, expose their cheap tricks.

What I also liked about Houdini was that, like me, he was loyal to friends. When he first started in show business, he worked in freak shows and even pretended to be a freak called the Wild Man. He would growl and tear at raw meat, and the audience would applaud and throw him cigars. But after Houdini left that gig, he never forgot the people he worked with. He knew he had only pretended to be a freak while the real freaks, like the Dog-Faced Boy or the Missing Link, were trapped in their weird-looking bodies, so he tried to help them whenever he could.

Houdini's freaks made me think of Old Man Jackson, and I told Jorge and Lucky that Jackson might be more normal if we made friends with him.

"Now *that's* a wack idea," Jorge said, looking at me like I just told him I'd been a girl in a past life.

But I think Jorge might have changed his mind if he had gone back to Jackson's with Lucky and me.

INSIDE JACKSON'S HOUSE: PART ONE

After school on Monday, I met Lucky in front of Jackson's house. We stood around, hoping he'd come out. We even would've been happy if Da Nang bolted through the front door, making one of his famous charges. But nothing happened. I thought I saw a silhouette in the upstairs window but couldn't be sure.

"Maybe the vet put both of them down," Lucky joked.

"Maybe we shouldn't have come," I said.

"What are you afraid of?"

"What if he thinks we did it? If Da Nang's dead, he'll kill us."

"You have a point there, Houdini."

We were about to leave when I heard a low growl from inside the house. Then I saw Jackson peering at us from a downstairs window. Lucky waved for him to come out.

"What are you doing?" I said, grabbing his arm.

"Isn't that why we're here?"

Jackson hobbled outside in his usual outfit—a clean white T-shirt and dirty overalls. He was followed by Da Nang, who moved very slowly, like he was still sick. His one good eye looked glazed, while Jackson's were lit up like Christmas bulbs.

"What do you want?" he asked.

"We came to check on Da Nang," Lucky said.

"You mean, you want to know if Fatso killed him?"

"We didn't know anything about that," I said, explaining we saw Angel with the piece of meat but didn't figure it out until Sunday.

Jackson cut me off. "I don't blame you boys. You don't got a mean streak like Angel." He rubbed his head with his good hand, then looked suspiciously at us. "You sure there ain't anything else you want?"

Lucky spoke up. "We're going to tell the cops."

Jackson laughed. "The cops? They don't care. They're just like the government. No, no, no, I don't want you to tell no one. I'll take care of Angel. Maybe not this week or the next, but I'll get my chance." He knelt down and petted Da Nang. "They say he'll be okay. His brain got a little fried, but he'll get better. He's a good, old friend." He told us to pet Da Nang, and it was a big leap, but I leaned over the short fence and rubbed him under his collar while Lucky cautiously stroked his head. I wished someone had been there to take a picture because we would've become legends.

"You boys want a Coke or something?" Jackson asked.

Lucky and I didn't know what to say.

"Da Nang won't bite you," Jackson said, though we weren't worried about Da Nang.

I was about to make up an excuse when Lucky said, "Yeah, sure," and jumped the fence.

I reluctantly followed, half believing this would be my last day on earth. Lucky and I would disappear into Jackson's house where Da Nang would attack us while Jackson took a machete off the wall and chopped us into little pieces, which he'd cover with chocolate syrup and hand out next Halloween.

TEN URBAN LEGENDS ABOUT JACKSON AND DA NANG

1. Jackson is really Da Nang and vice versa. Jackson wanted to be meaner, so he made a deal with the devil. Now he can bite people.
2. Jackson was spotted at three a.m. walking past the liquor store with his head tucked under his arm.
3. Sometimes Jackson removes Da Nang's glass eye and looks at people through it. The next day those people get sick or die.
4. Jackson was once married to a witch who, every Sunday morning, would turn drug dealers still working the streets into rats.
5. Jackson got tired of being married to that witch and sealed her up in his fireplace.
6. Jackson cultivated worms in the basement that could eat your brain. At night Da Nang would spit a jaw full of them into the open bedroom windows of kids who teased Jackson.

7. Jackson keeps his severed arm in an empty saxophone case. At midnight he opens the case and lets Da Nang play with the arm.

8. A local punk once peeked into Jackson's house and took a picture of him. The next day he was going to show it to his friends but woke up blind, and the camera was missing.

9. Jackson's house has no toilet. All the goop just stays inside him.

10. If Da Nang bit you, he stole your soul, and every night you'd have to bring him the fingers of babies to eat. No wonder we were afraid of them.

"A LOT CAN HAPPEN TO A PERSON"

As we walked into Jackson's house, the smell of incense almost knocked me on my butt, but I was happy to see there were no body parts scattered around. In fact, the house was neatly kept. Jackson didn't have much furniture, but his worn hardwood floors were clean, though the ceilings and walls were cracked and water stained.

"What's your name?" he said to me.

"They call me Houdini."

"That's a crazy name."

"He was a magician."

"Well, maybe you can make that scaredy-cat look on your face go away. You think I'm going to eat you?"

So Jackson was a mind reader.

"Your brother was never afraid of me," he said.

"How well did you know him?"

"I used to pay him to help me around the house," Jackson said. "He'd always bug me about Vietnam, and I'd tell him stories. Those stories should've scared him, but instead he goes off and joins the Marines." Jackson shook his head. "The problem with boys like Franklin is that they want to save the world but the world don't give a damn."

"Yeah, I know" was all I could say.

"You guys want that Coke now?" Jackson asked.

"Is it in a can?" Lucky said.

"You think I'm going to poison you?" Da Nang growled but Jackson calmed him down.

"No, sir," Lucky said, then Jackson hobbled into the kitchen and came back with two cans of Coke.

"You don't need no glasses," he said, and we nodded.

I looked at an expanse of wall over a fireplace that had been bricked up. On top of the fireplace were a few trophies, and the wall was decorated with a number of glass-framed photos and a medal I assumed was his Purple Heart. There was also a large bookshelf built into the wall packed with paperbacks and hardcovers, and that surprised me. Some of the books looked new but the spines of others were cracked and faded.

"Come on, I'll show you," he said, pointing to the pictures and medals, "but don't go off and join the Marines like Franklin."

Lucky and I followed him to the fireplace. The trophies were Most Valuable Player Awards for playing football, though looking at Jackson, I found that hard to believe.

"Makes you want to laugh, don't it, Houdini, but a lot can happen to a person. These are pictures of the boys I served with," he said, pointing to photos of young guys around Franklin's age, hamming it up for the camera. "Most of them are dead or crazy." He didn't say it with sadness or anger, almost like he had looked at the pictures a thousand times and had become used to the tragedy. He unhooked the medal from the wall and tossed it to me. It was his Purple Heart, and it seemed to glow in my palm. It was heart-shaped with a gold border, etched with the profile of George Washington.

I handed back the medal, then looked at the books.

"They're mostly novels," Jackson said. "Don't look so surprised, Houdini. Did you think I couldn't read because I talk so bad?"

"Houdini's writing a novel," Lucky said.

"Is that true?" Jackson said.

I nodded.

"Good for you, boy. Real people don't get killed in novels."

We talked a little longer about his books, drinking our Cokes, and keeping an eye on Da Nang. Then we promised Jackson not to call the cops, and stood to leave.

"Do you mind if I say something?" Lucky said.

"Let 'er rip," Jackson said.

"If I was you I'd cool it with the incense. Gregory might have you raided if he thinks you're smoking pot."

Jackson smiled. "No pot here, boys, and don't worry about Gregory. I ain't afraid of some moron with the same first and last name. What kind of parent would do that to a kid?"

Outside, as we walked away, I noticed our mountain of leaves across the street. It had grown to about eight feet high and twelve feet wide at its base. We only had a few houses left to rake this Saturday, and on Sunday we planned our diving contest, hoping to close down the business until next fall.

WAR

Unlike Jackson, Houdini thought it was an honor to go to war. In 1917, when America entered World War I, he wrote to a friend: "I register tomorrow for enlisting. Hurrah, now I am one of the boys." But the Army rejected him because he was too old—forty-three. He still did his bit, though, giving free performances for soldiers in training.

Listening to Jackson that day made me think Houdini hadn't missed much. It also made me wonder if Franklin was blown away by what he was witnessing in Iraq, or if the Marines got recruits used to seeing people killed by showing them films. Maybe that's why Franklin never answered my questions about war. My father and I would watch tanks and buildings getting blown up on TV, and we'd see pictures of wounded civilians or people whose amputated limbs had healed, but never a word from Franklin about any of it. We'd sit there pretending Franklin wasn't part of this misery, as if he was at summer camp. Of course we knew better, but it was easier for my father to focus on trying to keep his job and for me to do battle with Angel than to think of Franklin dodging bullets.

Meanwhile, my mother just kept baking, working at the cleaners, and studying her legal secretary books. One night she came into my room when I was writing, wanting me to show her the find/replace function of our word-processing program. She looked at the screen.

"Can I read what you're writing?" she asked.

"It's all junk," I said.

"I'm sure that's not true."

"If you read it, you'll change your mind."

"What kind of book is it?"

"A novel."

"Is it about us?"

"Kind of," I said, promising I'd let her read it when it was finished.

"What are you going to do with it when it's done?"

"I'm not sure," I said, starting to feel embarrassed.

"Well, all that matters is that you're having fun."

"But I'm not."

"If that were true, you wouldn't keep writing."

"You sure about that?"

She smiled. "Yes, just trust in yourself."

I stood and she sat down at my desk. "Before we start,"

she said, "can I ask you a question?"

"Sure."

"Angel's mother said kids call you Houdini Weenie. Is that true?"

"Just jerks like Angel."

"Does it upset you?"

"No, it's kind of a joke now."

"Good. You know, I try to be fair to Angel, but sometimes it's not easy. He's got a lot of anger for someone so young."

"Tell me about it," I said.

IN THIS CORNER

Although we promised Jackson not to tell the cops, we weren't going to let Angel off the hook. Still, we had to do something without telling Jorge because Lucky was right. Jorge would've flipped out, not because he loved Da Nang, but because he hated Angel. Fortunately, Jorge got detention the next day for swearing at some kid, so Lucky and I cornered Angel and his friends at a playground a couple hundred yards behind school. We said if he didn't stop messing with everyone, we'd spill the beans.

He just laughed. "You can't prove anything. Everyone hates that dog, anyway. I didn't poison him. I wouldn't kill an animal."

"That's not what Jackson believes," Lucky said.

"I don't care what Jackson thinks. It was just a rotten piece of steak I found in a garbage can behind my house. It's not my fault if it had something else in it."

"You still knew it'd make him sick," Lucky said.

Then one of Angel's friends interrupted him, this tall, bony guy with long, brown hair and sunken cheeks. He said his father was a lawyer and that Angel didn't do anything illegal.

"Shut up, goofball," Lucky said, and the kid backed down.

But Angel wouldn't let up. "And remember, Weenie Boy, who your pathetic mother works for."

And there was that threat again, which normally silenced me, but the word "pathetic" triggered something in my brain. I felt an electric twitch in my left cheek right before I punched Angel in the mouth. Unfortunately, he didn't go down, which freaked me out a bit.

Lucky was between us in a second, but I told him to back off. I was prepared to hit Angel a thousand times if I had to. I'd be fine as long he didn't pin me and snap my neck like a chicken bone.

Lucky shook his head. "You sure, Houdini?"

"Yeah," I said, though I really wasn't.

Then something surprising happened, something miraculous: Angel didn't want to fight, though it was clear he wasn't afraid, which spooked me even more. Instead, he pointed his finger at me and said, "Later, Weenie Boy, later." Then he walked away, followed by his pals.

"What was that about?" I said, standing there, shaking all over.

"I guess you really are Houdini," Lucky said, "because you just escaped a very serious beating."

"So why didn't he fight?"

"Good question," Lucky said.

THE IMPORTANCE OF BRAINS

The next day after class I stopped by the cleaners to say hi to my mother. She was standing behind the counter, dwarfed by a pile of dirty shirts she was separating. Overhead, I could hear Greek music coming from two small speakers set up in opposite corners of the room. At first the music was bearable but if I had to listen to it all day (and Angel's mother always had it blaring) I would have gone nuts. It ticked me off that my mother had to work here and I wondered what would happen if my father lost his job. Would he end up handling people's laundry or cleaning toilets?

When my mother saw me, she smiled.

"Hi, John," she said. Her hair was tied back, which made her face and blue eyes seem even rounder and larger than they were, and she wore one of Franklin's green Marine T-shirts. It wasn't a very attractive outfit, but I guess it made her think of him, and why bother getting dressed up if you work at a cleaners?

"It's hot in here," I said.

"It's always hot in here," she responded, laughing.

That's when I heard a door closing from somewhere in the back, and Angel's mother appeared. She seemed to have been born with a scowl on her face, and she had a habit of placing her hands on her hips and sighing when she got angry, which she was now.

"I'm gonna fire that tailor if he's late one more time," she said.

"But he's a good tailor, Olivia," my mother said. "He's just a little old."

He actually wasn't old. He was ancient. I guess he was a legendary tailor at one point, but now he chain-smoked and his hands shook so badly I was surprised he didn't stitch his fingers to whatever he was working on.

Angel's mother shook her head from side to side with such force I thought she was going to lose the pound of makeup she had plastered on. She was a short, fat woman who didn't know she was short and fat because she always wore tight miniskirts and brightly colored blouses that clung to her, exaggerating her potbelly. "If you owned this business, Sarah," she said, "you wouldn't be so forgiving."

My mother smiled and winked at me, and Angel's mother said, "Have you seen Angel?"

No, Mrs. Goofball, I wanted to say. "No, Mrs. Dimitri" is

what I actually said.

"The lazy bum was supposed to stop by after school to do a few chores."

He's also an idiot, I wanted to say. "I wouldn't know about that" is what I actually said.

"No, I guess you wouldn't. Angel tells me you don't like each other."

I didn't know what to say to that, but I didn't have time to respond, anyway, because I heard a buzzer go off, signaling someone had entered the store. It was Angel.

"Damn," he said, looking at me.

"Where were you?" his mother said, then added, "And don't embarrass me with your dirty mouth."

"With friends," Angel shot back, obviously upset his mother was giving him a hard time in front of me.

"With friends," she repeated. "Just like your father, always with friends, and while you guys are 'with friends,' I'm paying the bills."

Now *I* was starting to feel uncomfortable, even a little embarrassed for Angel. His mother was breaking an unspoken rule: you don't put down your kid in front of another kid.

"I have to go," I said to my mother.

Angel looked relieved.

"Yes, you go," Angel's mother said, beginning to tremble

a bit, her huge breasts threatening to burst the top button of her blouse. "You probably have leaves to rake while my Angel bum can't show up to do one lousy chore."

"I'll see you at home," I said to my mother, walking toward the door.

"Okay, John," she said.

Right before the door closed behind me, I could hear Angel's mother say to him, "Why can't you be like that boy?"

"All boys are the same, Olivia," my mother interrupted, trying to calm things down.

"What do *you* know?" Angel's mother said nastily, and I found it hard not to go back and tell her off.

On the long walk home, I felt agitated, angry at the way people treat each other. I couldn't stop thinking about something I had read the night before in a new biography of Houdini. Someone quoted him as saying, "My brain is the key that sets my mind free."

I think he meant that we should use our brains to make ourselves happy, or we'll end up miserable, like Angel's mother, who was so trapped by her nastiness, she'd forgotten how to talk or act decently. It was as if the same goofballs who had fiddled with Angel's brain had taken the Ginsu knife to hers, too.

TEN OTHER QUOTATIONS FROM HOUDINI

1. "What the eye sees and ear hears, the mind believes."
2. "Fire has always been and, seemingly, will always remain, the most terrible of the elements."
3. "My chief task has been to conquer fear."
4. "I always have on my mind the thought that next year I must do something greater, something more wonderful."
5. "No performer should attempt to bite off red-hot iron unless he has a good set of teeth."
6. "Magic is the sole science not accepted by scientists, because they can't understand it."
7. "I am a great admirer of mystery and magic. Look at this life—all mystery and magic."
8. "Nothing is more offensive to an audience than a performer to appear surly and bad tempered. He is there to please the public."
9. "My will has been stronger than my flesh. . . . I have

done things which rightly I could not do, because I said to myself, 'You must.'"

10. "The easiest way to attract a crowd is to let it be known that at a given time and a given place someone is going to attempt something that in the event of failure will mean sudden death."

I know a little something about the last quotation.

THE FIRST ANNUAL LEAF-DIVING CONTEST

Sunday, as planned, Lucky, Jorge, I, and about eight other kids, including Angel and his two cronies, gathered at noon in the field near the basketball courts. It was the first day of November, cool, cloudy and damp, like a hard rain was coming. But it was also invigorating, a good day to hurl yourself into a pile of leaves. The three of us brought our rakes and worked along the outer edges of the pile, tossing leaves onto its top, trying to create a huge pyramid. We also fluffed up the remaining leaves to provide more of a cushion so we'd disappear when we landed.

While we were working, Fiona Rodriguez and three of her friends came by, staring at us from the sidewalk with their arms crossed. Fiona was tall and thin with caramel-colored skin and big, dark brown eyes. Her blue jeans clung tightly to her behind, and I thought if she and Lucky ever got married their kids would look like movie stars or be

Olympic athletes. We all stopped shoveling leaves, waiting for her to say something, but she frowned and headed down the street, her friends following her like little puppies.

"That's one good-looking girl," Lucky said, and then we went back to work.

When we finished, Lucky decided to go first, then me, then Jorge, then whoever wanted to. One goofy kid had brought nine cardboard signs, three numbered 1, three numbered 2, and three numbered 3. The idea was to take turns having three different guys judge the jumps, deciding whether they deserved a 1, 2, or 3, so that the perfect jump would get a 9, the next perfect an 8, and so on. At first the idea seemed stupid, but it ended up being fun because everyone would yell out the number when the judges raised their cards.

We set up a garbage can next to the shed, and Lucky used it to climb onto the shed's roof. He scanned the crowd and said, "My friends, let the games begin." Then he swan dived, disappearing into the pile. Even Angel laughed as the leaves floated in the air above Lucky. Three kids lifted signs, adding up to 7. Not bad.

After Lucky crawled from the pile, we rebuilt it and I mounted the shed. I decided to cannonball, surprised when I hit the leaves because I expected a cushion that never came. For a moment I thought I might shatter my kneecaps, but eventually the shock of my fall was blunted by the middle of the pile. My dive received an 8.

The contest went on like this for about a half an hour. Jorge was the only one who received a perfect score for an insane running somersault. We froze when his skinny frame hit the leaves, but he came up swearing, like he had just jumped I-95 on a motorcycle.

Angel bowed out of the first round. Instead, he stood around insulting everyone, and I noticed him looking strangely at me when it was my turn. He hadn't forgotten I punched him, so I wondered what he was thinking. Finally, someone called Domino's, and twenty minutes later a guy dropped off five cheese and pepperoni pizzas. We walked down to the basketball courts to chow down, but Angel said he'd stay behind and rebuild the pile. He also said he'd jump when we got back. We couldn't figure out why he was being nice, but his absence meant more pizza, so no one complained.

When we returned, the pile seemed higher than before and it appeared to have been moved four or five feet to the left. Angel was standing on the shed, waiting for us. "How about a contest between me and you, Weenie Boy?" he said. "One jump apiece, to be judged by those guys." He pointed to three scraggly neighborhood kids.

I accepted his challenge, thinking that, because of his

bulk, he'd fall lamely off the shed. But he surprised me, re-creating Jorge's somersault. He missed the middle of the pile and landed hard off to the right but he was up fast, limping a bit, while his two friends gave him a standing ovation. I wasn't surprised when the judges awarded him a 9.

The contest was over when the cardboard signs were raised because I wasn't crazy enough to try that move. I'm not that flexible. Realizing this, Lucky asked to take my place.

"No way," Angel said. "It's between me and him."

"What does it matter?" Lucky said

"It matters because I said so."

"The heck with him," Jorge said.

So Lucky climbed the shed, while Angel kept telling him to forget the whole thing, which seemed very strange, but Lucky had a special jump in mind. He stood on the roof as far back as possible and sprang forward high into the air, accomplishing the impossible: a double somersault. He landed perfectly, so we were surprised when he didn't move and when we heard a sickening groan.

ONE GOOD REASON NOT TO INVITE ANGEL DIMITRI TO A LEAF-DIVING CONTEST

Before we could reach Lucky, he crawled from underneath the leaves, grasping his left leg. His pants were torn and there was a huge gash in his calf. I'd never seen a wound so deep, so I ripped some fabric from his pant leg, tying the material tightly below his knee in order to slow the bleeding. Meanwhile, someone called an ambulance, and we sat for what seemed like hours before it arrived. The attendants were the two guys from Jackson's house, but this time they were very professional, replacing my tourniquet with a piece of plastic tubing. They cleaned the wound, then helped Lucky into the ambulance. His face was white, so I knew the wound was serious. When the ambulance drove away, Jorge and I stood there, silent. During all the commotion, Angel and the rest of the kids had drifted off, probably afraid the cops might show up.

We stared at the pile, then grabbed our rakes and waded through the leaves, throwing them to either side until we found what we were looking for. Midway down were three empty aluminum containers about a foot high and two feet in circumference. It seemed that Lucky's landing had crushed one, making it split open. Its jagged edges were covered with blood.

"Damn," Jorge said. "Why didn't we check this earlier? We're lucky nobody else got hurt. I guess Lucky earned his name again."

Jorge was right that we should've checked the pile, but he was wrong that we were lucky. There was no way we could've missed those containers with all our jumps, and that's when I told him about me and Angel, and how I knew Angel would get revenge.

"That's why he wanted you to jump," Jorge said. "What a jackass. But now it's his turn."

"But how can we prove it? This is too nutty, even for him."

"We don't have to prove nothin'," Jorge said. "We can take care of it ourselves."

A WORM OF AN IDEA

We thought Lucky would be patched up and gone by the time we arrived at the hospital, but he wasn't. A nurse said they wanted a specialist to inspect his leg, thinking there might be permanent nerve damage if it wasn't stitched properly inside, so Lucky had to wait around. But she also said we could spend a few minutes with him until the specialist arrived. She added that two people had already been there. Unfortunately, when we got to his room, one of those people hadn't left—Lucky's father. We could hear him yelling as we entered. His face was as red as his hair, his whole head about to explode. He smelled like a brewery, and sweat beaded on his forehead and fat cheeks.

"Why did they call me?" he asked. "What a dumb stunt!" He pointed his finger a few inches from Lucky's nose. "You'll never play football again. That's what they're going to tell you, you big jerk."

I could feel Jorge about to explode, so I grabbed his arm.

"I didn't call you," Lucky said. "They asked for my home phone number and you're always hanging around the house. Why don't you just leave me alone for once?"

His father started screaming again until some nurses came in and asked him to calm down. Then they told us to sit in the waiting room.

After Lucky's father left, Jorge and I opened the curtain to Lucky's cubicle and found him lying on his gurney. In spite of the argument, he looked groggy but glad we came. "What happened?" he asked.

"What do you mean, 'what happened?'" Jorge said in amazement. "Your old man just acted like a goofball. That's what happened."

"I mean, how did I get hurt?"

So I told him my theory about Angel.

"I think you're wrong, Houdini. Angel was already here, checking to see if I was okay. He looked pretty freaked out."

"He should've been freaked out," Jorge said. "He almost killed you."

"Maybe he just wanted Houdini to get a little banged up," Lucky said.

"Ain't that bad enough?" Jorge said.

After arguing for a while, we eventually agreed that whatever Angel's motives were, something had to be done. As we talked, a plan was forming inside my head. It was like watching a worm crawl out of its hole. I could see its head and a little bit of its middle but its tail was underground. Still, the head would be a good place to start. I was going to tell Lucky and Jorge my idea but then remembered that the real Houdini had once said to never prepare your audience for a trick, especially if you hadn't completely thought it out. The goal was to surprise everyone, even yourself.

NINE IDEAS FOR REVENGE ON ANGEL I DIDN'T USE, AND ONE CRAZY ONE OFFERED BY JORGE

1. Dump a handful of ants down his back when he nods off in class.

2. Tie him to a telephone pole and give Wiffle ball bats to the guys he used to whack.

3. Before he gets to the bathroom stall where he skips classes, rub the toilet seat down with Bengay.

4. Pay Fiona Rodriguez to smile at him all day, and then to scream when he comes on to her.

5. Smash the headlights on the crack dealer's Lexus and tell him Angel did it.

6. Send Angel a box of chocolates with Da Nang's poop rubbed on the bottom of each piece.

7. Take a cell phone photo of Angel on the can and email it to the entire eighth grade.

8. While he's wrestling, cut off the combination lock on his locker (my father has a tool), then replace it with a new one, and watch him spend hours trying open it.

9. At lunch give him a giant soda laced with two cans of Red Bull, and watch him spin out for the rest of the afternoon.
10. Burn down his mother's cleaners. ("Just kidding," Jorge said.)

"FOUND TO BE MISSING"

Whatever my plan was, it didn't matter because everything changed very quickly when I came home and discovered bad news.

My mother said she'd been trying to reach me all day on my cell phone, which I'd recently bought with money from our leaf business but I had left it at home, afraid I'd lose it while leaf diving. I could tell she'd been crying, and she asked me to join her in the kitchen.

"Where's Dad?" I said.

"In the backyard, smoking."

"Did Franklin die?"

"No, he's missing. He's been found to be missing."

Found to be missing? I let that phrase float around in my head. How can you be "found to be missing"? If you're "found," then you aren't "missing." I knew these were stupid thoughts, but they kept me from imagining Franklin dead.

"How can they lose a guy?" I asked.

"There was what they called a skirmish and he got separated. They said there's no reason to believe the worst, but they honestly don't know when they'll have information. They were pretty upset because one soldier called another on his cell phone, and that soldier put it on his blog, then the newspapers got it. They wanted us to know before people started calling."

"On a blog?"

"I guess things like that happen now. All I know is he's missing."

I sat stone still, and she started crying again. It was the first time I'd seen her weep and moan like that, as if someone had driven a nail into her forehead, so I hugged her, my arms shaking with each spasm. My father came in shortly afterward. He stared at us, then went back outside. He was angry, and when he got like that, he always wanted to be alone. To him, that was better than drinking or crying or smashing something.

When my mother calmed down, she tried to say the name of the city where Franklin was last seen but had trouble pronouncing it.

"Just write it down," I said. She printed the word "Mosul" on a yellow sticky note and handed it to me. "Mosul," I said to my father, when he returned from his cigarette. "That's the city where Franklin was."

"Who cares what the name of the city is? Obama promised he'd get everyone out of there and nothing's happening."

My mother shushed him, saying the president was doing the best he could.

Finally, everyone settled down, and we ended up in separate rooms: my mother in the kitchen making dinner, my father on his recliner watching CNN, and me in my bedroom, where I stared at Franklin's bed. I grabbed the football he'd given me and tossed it from hand to hand. Then I went to my desk, and Googled Mosul. I found a site having nothing to do with the war, which was good because I didn't want to think about war. I wanted to know about the city—how large it was, what the people ate, how many churches and schools there were, what language they spoke, what god they worshipped. I needed to believe Franklin would fall into the hands of a family who hated war as much as we did.

Mosul was about 250 miles northwest of Baghdad. I learned that the fabric "muslin" was manufactured there and that the population was 1,800,000 people, and that the mayor's name was Zuhair Mohsin Mohammed Abdulazeez (no kidding). I learned that the people spoke Turkish and Armenian and Iraqi and Arabic, and that in the seventh century, Mosul was the capital of Mesopotamia, an area where the Tigris and Euphrates rivers met. In ancient times, it was real famous, kind of like New York City. I also discovered that

Mosul had the most Christians of all the Iraqi cities and that many of its artists specialized in paintings called miniatures. None of this information made me feel great, but it was better than going to the bathroom and puking.

When I shut down the computer, I lay on my bed, reading Franklin's most recent letter. I had written him about our leaf business, boasting that when he returned I'd take him to the best restaurant in Providence, making sure it had peanut butter cookies. I also said there'd be a happy ending to his stay in Iraq and that he'd return a hero. He had sent back one of his usual short responses: "Staying alive here, Scout. There are no happy endings. Just endings." At first I was confused by that last sentence, but now it was beginning to make sense, as if he knew the rules in Iraq were different, and that any ending would be fine with him as long as he got home. Thinking about Franklin's words, I skipped dinner and fell asleep on top of my covers, fully dressed.

I woke up at three a.m., soaking wet. It was dark, except for the faint light of a streetlamp that made everything hazy. I opened my closet, searching for anything of Franklin's, but he had cleaned house before shipping out. I was about to close the door when I spotted something shiny in a corner. It was a grip strengthener Franklin would squeeze during football season, though he'd also work it whenever he was tense.

I picked it up and held it in my hand. It looked like an

old-style can opener, its grip coated with blue rubber and shaped to fit the fingers of a hand. At first I had trouble grasping it because after years of being punished by Franklin, the rubber was molded to his grip. Finally, I maneuvered my fingers into the grooves and squeezed tightly. As I did, I remembered the night before he left.

I woke just before daybreak and noticed he wasn't in bed. Halfway down the stairs, I spied him on the living room couch staring mindlessly into space, squeezing the grip over and over again. He wore just boxer shorts and I could see his chest muscles heaving as if he were trying to catch his breath. He looked surprised when he saw me, but then smiled.

"What's up, Scout?" he said.

"You okay, Franklin?"

"Just a little nervous. You should go back to bed."

"Nervous" wasn't a word I'd ever heard Franklin use, so I asked if I could help.

He smiled again. "How about something to drink?"

I nodded and went to the kitchen, where I poured a glass of orange juice. When I returned, I handed it to him. "Do you mind if I stay?" I asked.

"Thanks," he said, "but I need to be alone."

"Sure," I said, slowly climbing the stairs, glancing back at him on the way up.

Remembering that night, I continued to squeeze the

grip, then lay down on my bed, sliding it under my pillow. I stared at Franklin's bed, and for a second I thought I saw him, his hands locked behind his head, his feet crossed. Did that mean he had died? Was he coming back to say good-bye?

I shook myself half awake, then went to my computer. I tried to write but couldn't, so I went to his bed and crawled under the covers. Lying there, I could feel the soft mattress give in to my weight, and I thought of our years spent together in this room, talking and sleeping.

That memory got me through the night.

"GET YOUR BEHIND IN HERE, BOY"

It didn't take long for the bad news to spread.

"People need dead heroes to take their minds off their stupid lives," my father said.

"Don't ever say that again," my mother yelled. "I won't hear about Franklin dying in this house."

My father apologized, but he was right, and in the morning, just as the Marines had warned, we received phone calls from the newspaper and local TV stations. My father explained it was a family matter, but one of the callers persisted.

"I think I gave you my answer," he said, his face tightening, "and if you come here with cameras, I'll freaking destroy them."

I looked at my mother, who decided to let the language slide.

It was clear the newspapers wanted something shocking or quotable, because their morning story had been short, even though Franklin's Marine picture took up a tenth of the page. Two months ago, who would've thought Franklin and I would've been in the newspaper unless we had robbed a bank?

That day, we stayed home, glued to the TV. I don't know what we expected, since CNN seemed more interested in some politician who'd cheated on his wife for the tenth time.

"Isn't everyone sick of that guy?" my father said.

As the day wore on, we wandered around the house, trying to avoid each other as much as possible. Lucky and Jorge called, but I didn't have much to say, except to ask Lucky how his leg was. He said he'd have to use crutches for a week, then maybe a cane, but there'd be no permanent damage. I hung close to home for the rest of the day, waiting for more details, which never came.

Early in the evening I got pretty upset and decided to Google every site I could find on the war, hoping to discover a recent picture of Franklin eating at a mess hall or playing football. I couldn't stop imagining him lying dead or being tortured. I felt like my head was going to explode, so I put on my Nikes and snuck out of the house, running aimlessly up and down neighborhood streets, not realizing all I had on was a pair of jeans and a T-shirt.

I ended up on a metal bench near the basketball courts, which were always lit to keep kids from doing anything nasty. I was panting, steam pouring out of my mouth. Sitting there, I thought I must've looked like some hyped-up druggie. I looked around, thinking I was only about five when Franklin took me here to shoot hoops. He wasn't great in basketball, but he was good enough to start. At five, I couldn't even reach the basket, but he worked on my shot, teaching me to use my legs and follow through. I would have given anything to go one-on-one with Franklin now, body up against him, feel us breathing hard as we tried to juke past each other. I stood and moved quickly around the basket, pretending to shoot jumpers with an imaginary ball. I could feel tears freezing on my cheeks, and I probably would've stayed there all night if not for someone shouting, "Houdini, what are you, nuts?"

It was Old Man Jackson leaning against his fence, Da Nang standing at his side. He pointed to his open front door, light streaming out onto the front yard. "Get your behind in here, boy, or you're going to freeze."

INSIDE JACKSON'S HOUSE: PART TWO

I wiped my tears and jogged toward the light, relieved to be out of the cold. In spite of the temperature, my shirt was wet with sweat. Jackson told me to take it off, then disappeared, returning with one of his own. "Throw this on while I make you something. All I got is coffee. Do you get hyper on coffee?"

"No, I can drink it," I said, sitting on an old couch by the bricked-up fireplace. Da Nang joined me, licking the back of my hand, then lying down next to my feet. I rubbed him under his collar until Jackson returned and handed me the coffee.

"I put cream in it. A boy shouldn't drink coffee black."

I nodded, though I had no idea what he meant.

We sat quietly, then I touched Da Nang's collar and asked how the contraption worked. He tossed me the control box. "Press the red button and see."

"I don't want to hurt him."

"Just do it," Jackson said.

"I can't."

Jackson grabbed the remote and manically pushed the button, laughing crazily. I waited for Da Nang to start bouncing off the walls, but he never budged.

"You mean it's fake?"

"Of course it's fake, Houdini. You think I'd zap Da Nang's brain? When I want him to stop, I snap my fingers like this," and he showed me, "and that's our sign. Everyone's so scared they don't pay no attention to me." He laughed loudly. "Now what were you doing out there? Did you have a fight with your parents?"

"Franklin's missing."

"He's dead?"

"No, he's missing."

"How can those morons lose people with all the electronic gizmos they have?"

"Good question."

He rubbed the top of his head. "Well, at least he ain't dead."

"We don't know that yet."

"But we do," he said. He stood and walked over to the photos he had hanging on the wall, pointing to different soldiers. "Now, *he's* dead, and *he's* dead, and *he's* dead," and he went on and on, finally stopping. "But Franklin could be anywhere. War is crazy, Houdini." He sat down in an old wooden rocker across from me. "Does Franklin know you've been here?"

"No."

"Why didn't you tell 'im?"

"I never thought to."

"Do you know how we met?"

"No."

"I was at the market, the one Gregory leveled a few years back. I always knew how much I could carry with my one good arm, but after I left, I realized I'd forgotten Da Nang's dog food. So I went back and bought a big bag. When I grabbed it, all the other stuff kept falling onto the floor. Every time I picked something up, something else fell. Then, all of a sudden, this big kid's standing behind me, asking if he can help."

"Franklin?"

"Yep. But I'm suspicious because no one's ever wanted to help me with anything, and that's okay, because I like it that way. The next thing I know, Franklin has it all figured out, and we're both tramping back to the house. When we get here, I throw the stuff inside and say good-bye, but he doesn't move, just standing there, looking around. So I invite him in and get him a Coke, just like I did for you boys. That's when we got to know each other."

"What did you talk about?"

"Like I told you, he couldn't get enough of Vietnam.

At first, I didn't want to go back there, but then I kind of enjoyed it, like it was easier talking to him than those crazy shrinks at the VA."

"What was he like at my age?"

"Serious, real serious, like he was forty or something. It kind of worried me."

I took a sip from my coffee, while he grabbed a book off the shelf, tossing it to me. "He loved reading this," he said. "You want it? It's not about politics. It's about the soldiers, about the kind of guys they were."

"I don't want to think about war right now."

"Probably best," he said, replacing the book, then saying, "You better get home or your parents will be mad. Don't worry about Franklin. I was with a lot of guys in Nam and I always knew who'd make it and who wouldn't. I got a good feeling about Franklin."

I thanked him and asked for my shirt back.

When I got home, my mother was waiting for me, worried. She wrapped a blanket around me and made hot chocolate. I was going to tell her I'd just had coffee at Jackson's but decided not to. Still, I couldn't keep my mind from racing. I don't know if it was the news about Franklin or the caffeine. I probably would have stayed up all night, rolling around in bed, except at around nine o'clock we received another phone call—this one, anonymous.

RIP

When the phone rang, my father told us to sit on the couch while he grabbed the receiver. My mother and I searched his face for good or bad signs, but he appeared more annoyed than anything.

"Who's this?" he asked. Then, "What?" Then, "Where did you say it was?" Then he hung up.

"What happened?" my mother said.

"There's no news about Franklin," he said. "It's about something else. I'll explain when I get back."

"No, you'll explain now."

"Trust me," he said. Then he told me to grab my jacket. He wanted to take a drive.

We didn't speak in the car. We drove a short distance onto I-95 South, then veered off at the first exit, hopping back onto I-95 but in the opposite direction. As we approached an overpass, I saw the problem. Someone who'd meant well had hung a big white sheet over the high wire fence built to keep people from leaping onto the Interstate. In big letters that seemed to glow under the streetlights, we read: "RIP Franklin Smith, Providence's Hero." Underneath "hero," someone had painted a big, red heart.

"Damn," my father said, angling our Taurus wagon onto the ramp at the next exit and driving toward the sign. When we reached it, he parked on the overpass, causing a traffic jam. Cars were honking as we walked toward the sign, but it was too high to reach, and whoever had hung it had tied its top edges tightly. It was cold, and besides jeans and work boots, all my father wore was a black T-shirt and a New England Patriots cap. He surveyed the sign and scowled at the motorists, who were leaning half out of cars, screaming at us. He shook his fist at everyone and walked back to the wagon. I followed him, hoping no one would take a swipe at me.

"Get in," he said.

I thought we were heading home, but instead, he backed up a few yards, then drove forward onto the walkway, still blocking half the road. The cars kept honking and lining up behind us, but my father ignored them. He grabbed a Swiss army knife from the glove compartment and told me to get out of the car. Suddenly, he was climbing onto the roof, slashing at the thick twine holding the sign in place. I tried to talk him down but he kept hacking away. He had just about completed his mission when the cops pulled up. There was some conversation, a little swearing, then they made us follow them to the station.

TEN THINGS YOU CAN DO TO CALM DOWN YOUR FATHER WHEN HE LOSES IT, WITH THANKS TO THE THESAURUS

1. Zilch
2. Zero
3. Zip
4. Scratch
5. Goose egg
6. Nix
7. Nil
8. Blanko
9. Jack
10. Nada

In other words, NOTHING. Just stay out of his way.

FAMILY REUNION AT THE POLICE STATION

The cops didn't question us much when they found out who we were. They almost seemed annoyed they had to bring us in, and one young officer, whose name was Carlos Perez, asked if we wanted something to eat or drink. He kept calling my father "Mr. Smith" in a very respectful tone, and we discovered he had served in Iraq.

"Do you know Franklin?" my father asked.

The cop, a short but very powerful bald guy, said he'd been in the Army, not the Marines, and that he had played football against Franklin in high school. "He was pretty amazing," he said, "even when he was a sophomore."

So we all sat there chatting, like this was your basic Little League banquet until my mother arrived.

Wow! What an entrance she made. It was almost eleven o'clock, so I couldn't figure out why she got so dressed up. She had on her camel overcoat, and when she removed it, she was wearing her favorite church dress, a nice blue number that broke above her knees. She also wore stockings and dress shoes. It's hard to think of your mom as being good-looking, but I guess she was, because a number of cops glanced her way. Did she think she'd be able to spring us faster if she came dressed up? It was a bizarre concept. Even more bizarre, she seemed to be crying and laughing at the same time. She walked right past the cops into my father's arms, and I stood there dumbfounded as she hugged him.

"How did you get here?" my father asked. But she didn't answer.

"Franklin called," she said. "They let him call. It was all a mistake, some kind of 'miscommunication,' they said. But he was wounded."

"Wounded?" my father said, and the young cop asked where.

"In the arm, but he's okay. He's coming home."

She tried to go on but broke into tears. My parents kept hugging each other, and I found myself jumping up and down, while the cops looked on, glad to make the charges go away. Before we left, Officer Perez gave my father his phone number and said, "Tell Franklin to call me if he wants to talk."

"About what?" my father said.

"Just tell him I served there," the cop said.

We didn't get home until about midnight, and my father

phoned his foreman to explain why he missed his shift. Although exhausted, we were all having trouble coming off the rush of the good news. My mother made some hot tea and put a plate of peanut butter cookies on the kitchen table, which made my father laugh.

Afterward, while she cleaned up, my father left to have a smoke. I found him in the backyard, sitting on a beach chair in his winter coat. It was cold and windy, but a full moon lit up the backyard. I didn't know what to say, so I sat on the cold ground next to him.

He lit another cigarette from the one he was holding and said, "If I ever catch you smoking, I'll knock your head off." He smiled and rubbed the top of my head. "Sometimes, it's hard, you know."

"What's hard?"

"Everything. Working, the bills. Just getting by. We have to do right by her," he said, motioning toward the kitchen. He took a drag from his cigarette. "Do you know about your grandfather's brother? His name was Dick."

"Just that he was killed in Vietnam."

"Franklin was always asking about him. He even used to do school reports on the war, and I think that's one reason he enlisted."

"Franklin never mentioned him to me," I said.

"Dick was about fourteen years younger than your

grandfather, kind of like you and Franklin. He was one of those guys who was class president, and everyone figured he'd be rich. But then he decided to sign up for Vietnam, and in '69 he was killed when he went back to help some guy who got shot. They gave him a Purple Heart even though he was dead, and something called the RVN Cross of Gallantry. That was supposed to make everyone happy, but it didn't. I haven't stopped thinking about him since Franklin left."

I wanted to say something but I wasn't used to my father talking about serious things.

He took a long drag on his cigarette. "I went with your grandfather to the Vietnam Memorial in Washington when I was about twenty-one, the year before I married your mother."

He glanced up at the sky, then all around him, as if someone might be listening. "At first, it seemed pretty stupid, just a black granite wall, about ten feet high, with thousands of names etched into it. I thought if I'd been asked to build something for all those dead guys, I could've come up with a better idea. It didn't take your grandfather long to find Dick's name because they're listed by the year they were killed. He was doing fine until he put his finger on the name. It was scary because he knelt down and almost fell over, like someone had shot him in the back. Then he cried harder than I've ever seen a guy cry. When I touched him, he pushed me away, but when I tried again, he hugged me, and I started to cry too. After that day I promised myself I'd always have his back."

He looked up, then rubbed the back of his hand across my cheek. "Why are you crying?"

"I don't know," I said, resting my head against his shoulder.

A WHOLE NEW ENEMY

Before that night, I'd never heard my father say much about death, and I hated thinking about it. Sometimes at two or three in the morning I'd wake up worrying about Franklin, and my stomach felt like it was soaking in battery acid. The fear of what happens after I die doesn't freak me out. The spooky part is the thought of nothing: no family dinners, no friends, no nothing.

Houdini liked cemeteries and he was often photographed in them. It makes sense that a guy whose job it was to cheat death didn't seem afraid of it. He probably got a rush every time he finished a routine, knowing he had shot death the finger. He even created an act where he was placed in a wooden box that was covered by dirt. Once in California, buried four feet underground, he couldn't breathe and started to flip out, which was the worst thing he could've done, because it made him use more oxygen. Fortunately, he managed to claw his way to the top, and he swore he'd never do that trick again.

Some writers put down Houdini, saying he was arrogant because he believed he was immortal. But if that were true, he wouldn't have planned his escapes so carefully. And even if he didn't seem afraid of dying, he once wrote that he always worried about his wife, Bess, going before him. He also kept a little journal of other relatives who had died.

People certainly thought of death differently during Houdini's time. I remember overhearing my mother talking to Franklin about a project he did in college on the Plague. She said that even a hundred years ago, people didn't live as long as we do. Sometimes you couldn't even count on babies making it through the first few years. People also died of tuberculosis and other diseases we have cures for.

With Franklin being wounded, death suddenly became more real. It was like a whole new enemy had popped up, one a lot more frightening than Angel Dimitri.

NO EXPLANATIONS

The next morning, we found out Franklin had indeed been missing, then mysteriously reappeared with a few other marines, though we never got the whole story.

"It's your kid," my father said, "and they tell you squat."

But we did learn that although Franklin's wound wasn't crippling, it was bad enough for him to come home, at least for a while. We were torn between the fear that he'd been wounded and our happiness that he'd soon be sitting at the kitchen table having dinner.

My father, probably thinking about his uncle, was still mad the Marines had unnecessarily worried us. They never apologized, but instead kept saying Franklin would receive a medal. "A medal?" my father yelled, back to his old self. "Who cares about a freaking medal?" That's when my mother ended her grace period on swearing, but she did it in a nice way.

We were all standing in the kitchen, my father leaning

against the sink, cradling a cup of coffee. My mother gently reached for his cup, placing it on the counter. She hugged him and said, "All that matters, is that he's coming home."

"I guess you're right," he said, returning her hug.

I think she was also glad we didn't end up in jail. But, whatever, we all knew we'd sleep better for the rest of the week, and that we could go back to our routines: my mother to the cleaners and her classes, my father to his job, and me to my friends and my plot to get revenge on Angel.

THE WORM CRAWLS OUT OF ITS HOLE

The next school day I was looking forward to being with Lucky and Jorge, hopefully doing something normal. Walking down the hallway toward class, I wasn't surprised to see Lucky on crutches, wearing a soft cast around his calf and foot. He gave me a playful poke with one of his crutches and congratulated me on Franklin coming home, but he looked tired and sad. When I asked Jorge about it, he said Lucky's father had threatened to kick him out of the house, repeating how dumb it was to start a leaf-raking business, even dumber to get hurt jumping into a pile of leaves, especially when the stunt would ruin Lucky's football career.

"But Lucky doesn't care about football anymore," I said.

"Yeah, but you know how it goes."

And I did. You could be a serial murderer in my neighborhood but if you were good at basketball or football, everyone cut you slack. Guys who never said boo to their sons would appear mysteriously at games, like they spent their whole lives teaching them how to play. The irony was that Lucky was probably a great football player because he thought about his father when he ran over people.

"Have you seen Angel today?" I asked.

"No."

"Are we still on for Saturday night? You sure your mother won't be home?"

"She's going away for the weekend," Jorge said, leaving out the "with some guy" part.

"You mean she's leaving you alone?"

"Why do you care? She's not going to be home, okay?"

"Sorry," I said.

"There's nothing to be sorry about. I take care of myself just fine."

Which was pretty much true. Most kids his age would've been in juvie if they had his life.

"Have you decided what we're going to do to him?" Jorge asked.

I was so tired from the craziness over Franklin's disappearance that, in a way, I didn't care as much about Angel. But something had to be done, so I told him my idea, which had crawled out fully formed from its wormhole that morning on the way to school.

He laughed and said, "I don't think he'll show up. He hates us."

"Don't forget, we all used to hang with each other."

"But that was a long time ago."

"Well," I joked, "then maybe he'll come because he wants to be cool like us."

"Dude, I don't even want to be cool like us."

TEN THINGS THAT MAKE YOU HIP IN MY NEIGHBORHOOD

1. Playing football
2. Playing basketball
3. Getting Fiona Rodriguez to look your way
4. Throwing a string of lit firecrackers into the yard of the local crack house at two o'clock in the morning
5. Getting Fiona Rodriguez to go out with you
6. Copping tickets for an Eminem concert, then talking your mom into letting you go
7. Throwing an egg at Mr. Gregory Gregory's car
8. Petting Da Nang without getting your hand bitten off
9. Being on the front page of the Metro section for cleaning the neighborhood of leaves
10. Getting Fiona Rodriguez to do more than just stare at you

So I guess, in some ways, Lucky, Jorge, and I were hip. But as far as me and Fiona went, forget it. She never looked my way.

THE STORM

Saturday night, a northeaster had come up the coast and was pummeling the neighborhood with a cold rain. Sewers were overflowing but, thanks to us, most of them weren't clogged by leaves.

Jorge, Lucky, and I got to the courts, taking shelter under a tree by the shed we had leaped from. Lucky and I wore slickers, but Jorge just had his hoodie on and was visibly shaking. "I hope that goofball gets here fast," he growled.

I offered to stretch my slicker over our heads like a tent, but he said, "Just leave me alone."

I asked Lucky if he had the razor, and he said yes.

"Do you think he's even going to show?" Lucky said.

"He'll be here. I told him if he wants a shot at Fiona Rodriguez, he'll have to be friends with us."

Jorge laughed and poked Lucky in the side. "She's only got the hots for one dude."

Lucky ignored him. "You sure he's going to fade into one

of those weird sleeps if we keep him up long enough?"

"If he falls asleep in class, by the time night comes, he's probably comatose. We just have to wait him out."

We all laughed at that, then we shivered under the tree for about five minutes until Angel arrived. He seemed nervous and smelled like booze.

"Am I late?" he asked.

"I told you five thirty," I said.

"You said six, Weenie Boy."

"Damn," Jorge said, "why are we bothering with this guy?"

"He's right, Angel," Lucky said. "If you don't stop the Weenie Boy stuff, the night's over."

Angel looked like he was ready to punch someone but backed off. "Yeah, yeah," he said. "I just thought Houdini said six."

"It doesn't matter," I said. "We have all night and we rented some video games with our leaf money."

"Cool," Angel said, as if he really meant it.

Then we hurried through the rain toward Jorge's house, which was only a block away while I kept reminding everyone to wait up for Lucky, who was still limping.

"CAN WE TAKE A HAND VOTE ON THAT?"

Jorge lived on the third floor in an old, beat-up, gray three-family, so we had to climb the hall stairs, ambushed by a strange mix of odors—boiling Italian sauce, old cat litter, and the stale sweat of a thousand people who had ever lived there. The stairs were covered with old paint cans, a headless doll, and a bunch of broken McDonald's toys.

The inside of his apartment would've been nice if someone had worked on it, though it wasn't dirty. It was more like no one lived or ate there, probably because his mother always bought takeout. And there was a huge, flat-screen TV on the living room wall, a gift from one of Jorge's mother's boyfriends, so we had a great place to play video games.

"When did you get that?" Lucky asked, pointing to the screen.

"About a month ago," Jorge said.

"Why didn't you tell us?"

"Why would I want you here?"

I took off my slicker and collapsed onto an old, black, soft, upholstered couch. Lucky sat next to me while Jorge went into the kitchen to pour us some sodas.

Meanwhile, Angel surprised us when he pulled out a pint of peach brandy from his jacket pocket. "You guys want some?" he said, trying to impress us.

Lucky frowned. "No thanks, dude. I'm already in enough trouble at home."

I said no, too.

"Suit yourself," he said, taking a gulp from the bottle.

Jorge returned, balancing four cheap plastic green glasses filled with Coke and squeezing a huge bag of potato chips under his arm. He handed the Cokes to everyone, and when he reached Angel, Angel showed him the bottle of peach brandy. "I'm cool," he said.

"Can we take a hand vote on that?" Jorge said.

We started on the video games, determined to play until Angel fell into one of his dead-man sleeps. Every time Jorge went back to the kitchen to refill the glasses, he'd smile and make a goofy face behind Angel's back, which made me laugh.

"What's so funny?" Angel asked.

"Nothing, dude, I'm just feeling happy."

Lucky, Jorge, and I took our time with our Cokes while Angel was knocking down his brandy like it was Powerade, not knowing he was making our job easier. If Angel was impossible to rouse after he fell asleep, then there was no way he'd wake up when asleep and drunk. We continued with the games, trying our best to laugh at Angel's jokes, but as the night wore on he got weird, talking about his lousy family, and saying no one ever gives him a break. The more tired and drunk he became, the more emotional he got. At one point, I thought he was going to cry when he mentioned his father's gambling problem. I actually liked the old Angel better. This new touchy-feely Angel was messing up our plan, and I didn't want to sympathize with him. Jorge seemed annoyed by the whole scene and motioned me toward the kitchen. When I got there he was mad. "Is that goofball ever going to pass out?"

"Just relax," I said.

"You know, my mother has sleeping pills around here."

"What, are you nuts?"

But Jorge wouldn't let the idea go, so we argued back and forth until Lucky came into the kitchen. "The dude passed out," he said.

"What?" Jorge said.

"The dude passed out. The last thing he said was 'Lucky, you're one of my favorite people.'"

Jorge laughed loudly.

I felt a great relief as we all went back to the living room.

Angel was half sitting, half lying on the couch. We sat on the floor, staring at him for a few moments.

"Where's the razor?" I asked, and Lucky reached into the pocket of his slicker, removing a brand-new razor and pack of blades. He'd also bought a can of shaving cream.

"Don't we have to lay him down first?" Jorge said, so we dragged Angel off the couch onto the rug.

Lucky poked him a few times in the forehead and shook one of his legs to make sure he was a goner.

"Who's going to start?" Jorge said.

BARBER SCHOOL

Unfortunately, we hadn't considered certain details. For instance, none of us shaved much, so we didn't have experience with razors, and instead of a professional electric one, Lucky had bought a Gillette Mach III blade.

"What do we do now?" Lucky said, holding the razor in his right hand and the shaving cream in his left. "Shouldn't we wet the Mohawk first?"

"Damn," Jorge said. "Who came up with this stupid idea, anyway?" Then he disappeared into the kitchen, returning with a pair of rusty scissors, a towel, and a bottle of Windex. He slid the towel under Angel's neck and sprayed his head with the Windex.

"Couldn't you have put water in the bottle?" I said.

"He doesn't know the difference."

After we wet Angel's Mohawk, Lucky chopped off chunks of hair with the scissors. It was tough going because the scissors were so dull. When there was only about a quarter inch of the Mohawk left, I saturated it with shaving cream, and Lucky went back to work, a little at a time, but his hand was shaky and the hair wasn't coming off easily. By the time he finished, the middle of Angel's head looked like the field by the basketball courts, mostly bare but spotted with ugly patches of grass.

Lucky sighed and slid the towel from under Angel's head, using it to wipe the remainder of shaving cream and black hair from his skull. We should've been laughing—that was the whole point—but you would've thought we had just removed his appendix.

"Don't you think we have to do more than shave his head?" Jorge said. "Tomorrow he'll just finish the job and people will think he did it to be cool."

"He'll still look like a goofball," I said.

"I agree with Houdini," Lucky said. "We've done enough."

But Jorge felt Angel needed more punishment, and he reminded us Angel could've killed Lucky, me, and Da Nang. We had finally told him about the rotten piece of meat.

"Dude, you gotta let it go," Lucky said.

"Why do you care about the guy?" Jorge said. "The jerk almost killed you."

Lucky got mad. "It's over, so let's get him home."

"You act like you hate the guy, but you're always cutting him slack."

"Jorge's right on that score," I added.

Lucky ignored Jorge, but got in my face. "Does your dad ever smack you, Houdini?" he said, poking his finger into my chest.

I pushed his hand away. "You know he doesn't."

"What would your mother say if he did? Would she let it slide, like Angel's mom and mine?"

I didn't answer.

We stood, facing each other, and I would've felt better if he didn't have the razor in his hand. "I asked you a question," he said, moving closer.

Jorge got in between us. "Cool it, Lucky."

Lucky shook his head at both of us. "You guys think you know everything, but you don't know squat."

Now Jorge was mad. "Gimme a freaking break. You want us to cry for poor Angel because his family sucks?"

"I just want you to let it go."

"I'll let it go," Jorge said, "if we get Old Man Jackson to come over and cut off his privates."

Which was a crazy idea but not completely crazy.

OLD MAN'S JACKSON'S HOUSE YET AGAIN

Moving Angel wasn't easy, especially since we had to carry him down two flights of stairs without killing him. When we got to the second floor, an apartment door opened and I heard a baby screaming in the background. A huge, pasty-faced guy stood in the hallway, holding a can of Bud Light. His long, black hair was tied into a ponytail and he wore a black wife beater and white boxer shorts patterned with red hearts. I almost laughed.

He smiled. "He ain't dead, is he, Jorge?"

"No, just sleeping."

"Sleeping?"

"Don't ask."

"I won't," the guy said, "as long as you're sure he's not dead. We don't need no dead guys around here. I don't want to move again." Then he went back into his apartment.

"What did he mean by that?" Lucky asked.

"Nothin'," Jorge said. "Let's just get Angel outta here."

The idea was to drag Angel downstairs and throw him into a wheelbarrow I'd seen leaning against the house. Next, we planned to haul him to Old Man's Jackson's house, lift him over the fence, pound on Jackson's door, and run away.

We picked a good night to wheel him down the street. It was only about nine o'clock but because of the storm, no one was out, and we knew that if anyone happened to see three kids, one limping with a cane, lugging a body in a wheelbarrow, they'd close their drapes and go back to their TVs.

Jorge held one handle of the wheelbarrow, and I held the other while Lucky walked point. Because Jorge was shorter than me, it was hard to steady the wheelbarrow. About halfway there, it tipped and Angel toppled facedown next to the curb, torrents of rainwater bathing his face.

"Damn," Lucky said as we lifted him back into the wheelbarrow.

When we arrived at Jackson's, we somehow lugged Angel over the fence, dragging him through the muddy front yard and propping him against Jackson's door. "Maybe we should put an apple in his mouth," Jorge said.

"Shhhh," I said, trying not to laugh.

I thought we should wait for Jackson, but Jorge said to let it be a surprise, and I could almost see Jackson's big grin when a sopping-wet Angel collapsed onto his living room floor. I imagined him staring at Angel, rubbing his hands together, as if someone just dropped off a Thanksgiving Day turkey, while Da Nang licked his newly shaved head like it was a piece of filet mignon.

My daydream dissolved when we heard Da Nang begin to bark. Jorge and I helped Lucky over the fence and we hustled back to Jorge's. I had to be home by ten, so I left, promising I'd call tomorrow after Mass. But what we all were secretly wondering was how Angel would get revenge at school on Monday.

TEN WAYS TO DESCRIBE ANGEL'S SHAVED HEAD

1. A hundred-year-old soccer ball
2. Mr. Potato Head after being stung by a hive of bees
3. An undercooked meatball
4. The moon after a meteor shower
5. A burnt Brussels sprout
6. A round piece of Swiss cheese with ants on it
7. A white jellyfish with a rash
8. A horse's ass with acne
9. A clam (That was Jorge's. Lucky and I didn't know what that meant, but Jorge couldn't stop laughing.)
10. A barber's bad dream (Mrs. Guido, the next week in class. Though she said it nicely.)

"VERY CREEPY"

On Monday, Lucky, Jorge, and I discovered Angel leaning against the school's flagpole, talking to his flunkies. His head was shaved to the bone, spotted here and there with tiny red scabs. Lucky was still walking with a cane, which was good. I figured that when Angel tried to kill me, Jorge and I could tackle him while Lucky beat him unconscious.

Surprisingly, Angel wouldn't even look at us, and when he did, he focused on me. I braced myself but was surprised when he asked, "How's your brother?"

"What?" I said.

"How's your brother?"

"He's coming home," I said, slightly stunned, as I walked off with Lucky and Jorge.

"What was that about?" Lucky said.

"Very creepy," Jorge added.

I had to agree that Angel's response to Saturday night was pretty weird, and I believed his revenge would come sooner than later. I figured the next time I turned my back—to open my locker or to take a drink from a water fountain—I'd feel the thump of a blunt instrument on my neck. For that whole week I didn't go anywhere without Lucky and Jorge.

And I was right that Angel pretended to have shaved his head on purpose, though Jorge was right that he looked like a meatball. But whatever happened that night seemed to have changed how he acted toward me.

So what *did* happen at Old Man's Jackson's?

Jorge believed Da Nang bit off Angel's privates because he was sure the pitch of his voice had gone up an octave.

Lucky thought Jackson held a gun to Angel's head all night, periodically spinning the chamber and pulling the trigger, or maybe, he said, it would be enough for Angel to wake up hungover staring into Da Nang's one good eye.

Whenever we asked Jackson he'd laugh and say, "The boy just needed to be educated. There's somethin' decent in everyone, even Angel."

"Fat chance," Jorge said.

THE ZOO

During the two weeks that we waited for Franklin to come home, we talked to him on the phone, so we weren't worried something bizarre would delay his return. It seemed like one day we heard he was leaving Iraq with a stopover in Germany, the next, Lucky was shaving Angel's head and I was watching my back, and the next, Franklin was sitting at the dinner table, eating peanut butter cookies with his right hand, his left arm suspended in a sling.

All I know is that it was cool to be with him again. Everywhere we went, people said hello or patted him on the back, and we could eat any place for free. At first, Franklin enjoyed the attention, though he was quieter, and he seemed to space out sometimes, like he was looking at something none of us could see.

He also didn't seem comfortable inside restaurants, and one time in the middle of lunch he surprised us when he left without saying a word. My father followed him outside and they spoke in the cold for about five minutes before returning. My mother and I sat in the booth, watching them through the plate-glass window, Franklin shaking his head while my father rested his hand on Franklin's shoulder. My mother told me not to ask questions, so we all pretended nothing had happened. But in spite of that day, Franklin seemed happy to be home, sleeping in his old bed, and I felt safer.

The Saturday after Thanksgiving, Franklin took me to the zoo. It was cold and sunny, and we got there at nine a.m. to avoid the holiday crowd. I hadn't been to the zoo in a while, and it had been fifteen years for Franklin. He was blown away by all the changes, a little disappointed the polar bear and his favorite deranged camel had died. When he was a kid, he and his friends used to tease the camel and it would spit at them.

Halfway through our visit, we grabbed some hot chocolate and huddled around a table outside the gift shop. He asked me how I was doing.

"Fine," I said.

"That's weird what Gregory's doing to Jackson."

He was referring to a march Gregory had organized on Jackson's house. Gregory had done things like this before. He'd stir up some nutcases, then magically appear in his Maxima and give a speech. I didn't see what Gregory could do to Jackson, but my father explained there were a lot of ways to force people out of their homes. Gregory was arguing that Jackson's house was a health hazard.

"Yeah, it's real wack," I said. "You know, Jackson said you used to go over there. Why didn't you tell me?"

"You were just a baby."

"He said you were always asking about Vietnam."

"I wanted to learn about where Uncle Dick was killed."

"Didn't he die way before you were born?"

"Yeah, but everyone was always comparing me to him. It makes you want to know more. You probably don't know much about him, do you?"

"Dad told me the story a few weeks ago."

"Really?"

"Yeah."

"Why?"

"He said he hasn't stopped thinking about Dick since you left."

Franklin seemed uncomfortable and took a sip of his hot chocolate. "You going to play football next year?" he asked.

"Maybe. Mom wants me to apply to the Catholic high schools that offer scholarships. She's heard it helps if you play sports."

"Is that what you want?"

"How would I see Lucky or Jorge?"

"Is that important?"

"Yeah."

"Then stay where you are. You're smart, so make sure you end up doing something using your head." And he asked what I wanted to be. I said I planned to talk our dad into opening his own cleaning business and then maybe Franklin could join us when he got discharged.

"Don't count on that right now. I'm supposed to go back."

"To Iraq?"

He nodded.

"Do you have to?"

He rubbed his wounded arm. "It's pretty complicated," he said. He looked like he was trying to catch his breath.

"They can't make you go, can they? I thought after you got shot, you came home, got paid a lot of money, and were a hero."

"Let's talk about something else, okay?"

"So I guess no family business then?"

"I'm not sure about anything right now. But we all expect you to go to college. There must be something you like besides working as hard as Dad. Mom told me you've been writing a book. What's it about?"

"I'm not sure yet, but we're all in it."

He laughed. "You're not going to embarrass us, are you?"

"I'd never do that, Franklin."

"I'm just kidding."

"You should write a book about Iraq," I said. "You were always smart enough to do anything."

"To be honest, I'd like to forget about Iraq right now."

"Then whatever you do, don't write a novel. Writing makes you think very hard about things."

"What do you mean?"

"Just describing things can freak you out."

"Really?"

"Like you getting wounded. Normally, I'd just tell myself, 'Franklin got wounded,' then try to distract myself by watching TV or shooting hoops. But if I start imagining it and describing it and writing about it, I get nightmares."

"Then why bother?"

"Because I usually feel better afterward."

"I don't get it."

"Neither do I."

"Well, if it makes you happy, then do it. Those old dead guys from our coat of arms would probably be proud of you."

"DON'T TELL ME ABOUT FAIR"

For the next few days after our zoo visit, I kind of stalked Franklin. Sometimes he seemed like the Franklin I knew, but other times he appeared stoned, like some alien had crawled inside his ear and was eating his brain. During those times he rarely smiled, and he'd leave the TV room when the news came on.

Once, I asked my father if Franklin had to go back when he was healed, and he said it wasn't clear yet, and that we'd "cross that bridge when we came to it."

"That wouldn't be fair," I said.

"Don't tell me about fair right now, John." He was talking about his job. It seemed like the inevitable layoffs were starting. We all thought his fifteen years with the company would give him security, but he wasn't so confident.

The biggest change I noticed in Franklin was at night. Even if he had a great day, he would roll around in bed during the early morning hours, talking to himself. Or he'd go downstairs for a while, return in ten minutes, then do the same thing one hour later. It kept me awake, but I never complained.

One Sunday at around two a.m., I heard voices, so I left my room and sat at the top of the stairs. Franklin and my father were talking in the kitchen, but it was hard to make out the conversation, so I crept down a few more steps. I probably should have gone back to bed but I was worried that my father had lost his job or that something was wrong with my mother and everyone was hiding it from me. I walked into the kitchen, where I found Franklin sitting next to my father, his head buried in both hands, crying. I had never seen a guy that age cry, and it scared me. Sensing my presence, they both looked up.

"What's the matter?" I said.

Franklin wiped the tears from his cheeks with both hands. "Just go to bed," he said, "I don't want you to see me like this."

I went upstairs and lay there for about an hour. When I heard Franklin and my father talking outside my room, I pretended I was asleep. Franklin came in, closing the door behind him. His bed groaned as he collapsed onto it. All was quiet, until he came over to my bed, sitting down on its edge and pulling the covers up to my chin. Then he placed his hand on my forehead and ran his fingers through my hair the way my mother does when I'm sick. It was very hard for me not to cry but I didn't want to make Franklin feel worse, so I lay quietly until he wandered back to his own bed and went to sleep.

The next day Carlos Perez, the cop who'd served in Iraq, showed up at the house, and he and Franklin went off together.

THE STUPID LAW

Mr. Gregory had his march on Jackson's house organized for noon on the first weekend of December. Although my father, Franklin, and I had talked all week about the stupidity of the event, we decided to make an appearance and see what Gregory was up to. I told Lucky and Jorge to meet us there at 12:30.

It was colder than usual that Saturday with periodic snow showers that didn't stick to the ground. Because of the cold, I was surprised to see about twenty lost souls marching in front of Jackson's house. They looked like a bunch of homeless people or drunks Gregory had paid to raise a stink. Some of the protesters held up a sign with THE COMMITTEE FOR BUILDING REHABILITATION printed on it. You didn't have to be a genius to figure out none of these people cared enough to write that. In fact, most of them were pretty quiet, trudging behind each other like convicts in a chain gang. Then Gregory arrived in his Maxima, followed by a van from a local TV station, and things picked up.

My father, Franklin, Lucky, Jorge, and I watched from across the street by the basketball courts. Gregory's entrance was very dramatic, as he leaped from his Maxima like Apollo Creed in one of those Rocky movies. He was dressed in a black topcoat and bright red scarf, and he raised his arms over his head, announcing his presence. In one hand, he held a megaphone and began shouting, "Jackson unfair, Jackson unfair." His crowd of stooges echoed the chant, and the TV people began shooting footage.

"What a jackass," Jorge said.

"Jorge, my dad's here," I warned.

"That's okay," my father said, slapping Jorge on the back. "Gregory *is* a jackass." That comment made Franklin laugh.

The demonstration went on for about five minutes, then Jackson and Da Nang appeared on the porch. Although it was freezing, Jackson didn't wear a jacket, like he wanted to show how tough he was. He placed a kitchen chair on the porch and sat on it, Da Nang at his side. He lit up a pipe, crossed his legs, and stared at everyone.

"Can't we do anything?" Lucky said.

"Gregory's not breaking any law," my father said.

"He broke the Stupid Law when he showed up," Jorge said.

"What law is that?" I asked.

"The law that keeps you from doing stupid or mean things. It's not written down, but everyone knows it."

Franklin laughed again. He crossed the street, and we followed.

At first Gregory didn't notice Franklin because he was dressed in street clothes, not his uniform, but then he saw Franklin's sling and rushed toward him, like he had just spotted his long-lost brother.

"Franklin, my man," he said. "I'm glad you're here. I know you love this neighborhood. And you brought my main men, the human leaf blowers." He thought this comment was extremely funny, and he laughed as he slapped Franklin on the back, which made Franklin wince. "Look, gentlemen," he said, "a real war hero."

"I'm not here to march," Franklin said.

"Oh, come on, man, just look at this house." Gregory had a point. No paint job could save certain sections of dilapidated clapboard, and many of the windows had spider-web cracks. You could also see rotting plywood on the roof where shingles used to be.

Gregory continued. "One way to change this neighborhood is to change the way people feel about it, and this house is a cancer."

"So you're saying if Jackson fixes up his house, everything

will be cool?" Franklin asked.

Gregory didn't know what to say to that, but Jackson, who'd been listening, did.

"I don't got no money to fix nothing," he yelled. "Mr. Two Names knows that." Then he left his chair and walked toward us, telling Da Nang to sit tight. When he reached Franklin, he leaned over the fence and, much to Gregory's disappointment, gave Franklin a playful jab in the stomach. "I'm proud of you, boy," he said. "At least you got to keep your arm." He and Franklin laughed.

"This isn't personal," Gregory said to Jackson.

"It isn't?" Franklin said.

"Oh, come on, Franklin. You know me better than that."

Franklin seemed annoyed. "What you're saying," he repeated, "is if Jackson fixes up his house, there'll be no problems?"

Gregory hemmed and hawed, then finally said, "I guess so, but the guy has no money."

There wasn't too much talking after that. Franklin asked Jackson not to worry, and he told the TV crew to come tomorrow if they wanted a story.

"You tell 'em, Franklin," Gregory said, very much pleased with himself.

To be honest, I was a bit disappointed in Franklin's response. I had wanted him to scream at Gregory or drop-kick him in the face. But it was time to go, so we left just as the Gregory brigade resumed its marching and chanting. We were about to turn the corner onto our street when I noticed Angel, half hiding behind a tree. When he saw me, he tried to disappear behind the trunk but he was too fat, and I wondered what he was up to now.

Instead of going home, Franklin said he wanted everyone to come back to the house. He was as pumped up as I'd seen him since his return. He said he had a plan to fix Jackson's house, but that it would cost money. That was fine with me, I said, as long as it didn't involve shaving every strand of hair off Mr. Gregory Gregory. My father and Franklin didn't know what to make of my comment, but Lucky, Jorge, and I had a good laugh.

ONE BIG HAPPY FAMILY

At first Jorge wasn't too crazy about helping Jackson. After all, he hadn't been inside Jackson's house with Lucky and me, or talked to him, so he hadn't seen Jackson's normal side. He asked Franklin, "Why bother?" and Franklin said, "Sometimes you have to make a statement." Jorge looked confused by that response, but he shut up anyway.

As much as Lucky, Jorge, and I needed the money we made raking leaves, we volunteered to throw fifty bucks into the kitty, and my father contributed a hundred more. But Franklin wouldn't let anyone pay. I guess he had a lot of cash saved because he certainly couldn't spend it while dodging bullets in Iraq.

We all piled into my father's station wagon and drove to Home Depot, where we purchased the tools and materials we needed. At 12:30 the next day, a truck was supposed to arrive at Old Man Jackson's and drop off everything. Franklin bought Lucky, Jorge, and me brand-new work belts that had special places for shiny screwdrivers, hammers, nails, and a utility knife. He also bought some plywood, shingles, paint, primer, and spackle. He said if it got too cold over the next few weekends, we could work on the inside. I had told him about the damaged walls. All night I played with my new tools, slipping my hammer in and out of its holster like a six-shooter.

The next day at one o'clock my father, Franklin, Lucky, Jorge, and I armed ourselves and marched like the Seven Dwarfs down to Jackson's house. Fortunately, it was a good ten degrees warmer than it had been yesterday.

"This is so cool," Jorge said, weighed down by his tool belt.

Lucky said, "I have a feeling Gregory won't be helping us with our leaf business next year."

"We don't need that goofball," Jorge said.

My father laughed, and Franklin said, "Don't worry, Gregory will somehow spin this his way."

Gregory didn't look very happy when a war hero with one good arm and a work crew arrived to fix up Jackson's house. Lucky was still limping, and Franklin confessed he wouldn't be able to do much, but he was aware how his picture would look in tomorrow's paper. So was Gregory. At first he seemed kind of stunned as the cameraman shot footage, and a hot, blond reporter interviewed Franklin. Then he told his stooges to go home and he hung around, leaning on his Maxima and watching us work. Jackson finally came out, saying, "Bless you. Bless you all," and, like the rest of us, he took orders from my father, who could fix most anything.

My father, Jorge, and I started by tearing off and replacing rotting clapboards while Franklin and Lucky scraped chipped paint off the sections that weren't ruined. Then my father and I climbed onto the roof and ripped off damaged shingles and plywood with crowbars. At one point, I took a breather and that's when I noticed Angel peering again from behind that same tree, that is, until he joined Gregory. *What a pair,* I thought.

"Go home, Angel," Jorge said.

"Let him alone, Jorge," Jackson said, surprising us. "You want to help, Fatso?" he added, smiling at Angel.

Angel hopped the fence and grabbed a hammer. "Just don't call me that, okay?"

"You got it," Jackson said.

I didn't feel too comfortable with Angel swinging a hammer behind my back, but we didn't need him for that, anyway. What we needed were two strong guys to saw and lift sheets of plywood up to my father and me. Angel was one of them. The other was Jorge.

"I ain't working with him," Jorge said.

"Take a hike," Angel said.

"No, *you* take a hike," Jorge said back.

This dissing went on for a few more seconds until Jackson told them to shut up or he'd have Da Nang eat them. Everyone laughed, and as I looked around, all I could think of was a big, red Super Duty 450 Ford truck I'd seen advertised on TV. On its side panel I imagined JOHN SMITH AND SONS: HOME IMPROVEMENT. Maybe I could sell that idea to Franklin.

Now I know what you're thinking. There's Mr. Gregory Gregory with the cameras rolling, watching this little drama play itself out, and what a perfect ending it would be if he tore off his topcoat, hopped the fence, and helped us. For a moment, I thought he might. He was fingering the top button of his coat, deliberating, but instead he smiled, slid into his Maxima, and drove away.

But Franklin was right. The next day in the paper, right beside a picture of us hard at work, was a short article where Gregory proclaimed he had seen the light. Of course, the way to rebuild the neighborhood wasn't to "search and destroy" but to fix it up, and he promised to start a fund for home improvements. He even said he'd do some of the work himself. I couldn't see him and Jackson working side by side, but it didn't matter, anyway, because he never showed up.

"You have to give it to that Gregory," my father said, "he doesn't miss a beat."

As far as Angel goes, I can't say we became best friends, but something changed. Although he still said stupid things, he didn't seem so nasty, almost like he was trying to make jokes and act the way Lucky, Jorge, and I do when we tease each other, hoping we'd all hang together again. During the next few weekends, he'd join us at Jackson's and we got to know him in a different way. That happens when you work with someone.

"He's just tricking us," Jorge said, though I think Jorge was wrong.

I also think my mother had something to do with Angel's change. Right around that time, I had noticed her going into work on her days off, and when I asked her about it she said she was helping Angel's mother to make improvements to the inside, even doing some painting.

"For free?"

"Yes, for free."

"Why would you do that?"

"Because, like everyone else, she's struggling, and if she goes bankrupt I won't have a job."

"At least the second reason makes sense."

"Well, I hope the first one does too, or I've done a bad job with you. You want to come with me?"

I told her I had made plans with Lucky, which was true, but that I'd walk her to the cleaners. When we arrived, I was surprised to find Angel there. He was trying to cut and tack wood paneling onto an old counter, something he wouldn't have known how to do before working at Jackson's. I asked him if he needed help, and he tossed me a hammer, telling me to nail while he held the paneling flush against the counter.

"Just don't hit my thumb, Weenie Boy," he said.

I was surprised and angered by his comment, but when I looked up, he was smiling, so I let it slide and stayed there until the job was done.

Who would've ever thought a few months ago that on a late Wednesday afternoon, Angel, me, and our mothers would've ended up working together like one big happy family.

Very, very weird.

TEN OTHER GUESSES ABOUT WHAT HAPPENED TO ANGEL AT OLD MAN JACKSON'S

1. Jackson drilled a hole into the back of Angel's skull and let Da Nang suck out the mean part of his brain. (Jorge.)

2. Angel woke with the hand from Jackson's severed arm choking him, and promised to stop being a lunatic if Jackson put it back into the saxophone case. (Me.)

3. Jackson whacked Angel over the head fifty times with the same slab of rotted meat that poisoned Da Nang. (Me again.)

4. Angel was abducted by aliens after he left Jackson's, but they couldn't stand his smell, so they turned him into a good zombie and sent him home. (Lucky.)

5. Jackson cut off Angel's privates, so he became one of those ostriches. ("They're called eunuchs, Jorge," I said, "and you already used the 'privates' thing." "Take a hike," he said back.)

6. Fiona Rodriguez appeared to him while he was sleeping and her saintlike smile tamed him. (Lucky.)
7. Angel finally started popping the right meds. (Jorge.)
8. Jackson's witchy girlfriend came back from the dead
   and spanked Angel with her broom. (Me.)
9. Jackson tied Angel to the kitchen chair, then took off
   his head and set it on the table, where it lectured Angel
   about being decent. (Lucky.)
10. Jackson threw Angel into a cold shower, then washed
    his clothes and made him coffee, and talked to him
    the way he used to talk to Franklin, and somehow
    convinced him not to be a jerk anymore. ("That's so
    freaking sappy," Jorge said.)

Maybe Jorge was right, but that's what I've decided to
believe.

"TAKE A PILL OR SOMETHING"

After that first day working at Jackson's, everyone went home feeling pretty good about themselves. Franklin and I probably could have ridden that high for days, except my father found out on Monday he'd been laid off. His boss said he was hoping it wouldn't be long, but I could see the shock on my father's face. It was as if someone had cut off his legs, and I realized there had probably never been a day since he married my mother when he didn't pack a lunch, fill a thermos with coffee, and go to work. Also, everything seemed worse because it was close to Christmas. I had a laid-off father, a brother who seemed sad and strange at times, and my mother was still working at the cleaners. I had always assumed people would take care of me, but now I wasn't so sure.

"It could be worse," Jorge said.

He, Lucky, and I were chilling at Dunkin' Donuts.

"He's right," Lucky said. "My father hasn't worked much in a year."

"But he wasn't fired," Jorge said, laughing. "He's just a lazy drunk."

Lucky could have pointed out that at least he knew who his father was, but to his credit, he didn't. I think he realized this was one of Jorge's hyped-up days, and when he got like that, he didn't filter much.

"So you're saying Franklin's depressed?" Jorge asked.

"I'm just saying he's having problems." I hadn't told them about the crying.

"I don't blame him," Lucky said. "Imagine the crazy stuff he saw there."

"I don't know," Jorge said. "I saw this movie about a guy coming back from Iraq. He killed some kid there by mistake, and when he came home, he went crazy and eventually hung himself."

Lucky whacked Jorge alongside his head. "Damn, Jorge," he said. "What are you, crazy? Take a pill or something."

Jorge finally got it. "Dude," he said to me, "Franklin would never do that. You know how I run off at the mouth."

"Forget it," I said, but the thought had crossed my mind.

When I got home my father was watching television and Franklin was out.

"Where's Franklin?" I asked.

"He went somewhere with Carlos." Franklin had been working out with Carlos at the YMCA, and although he couldn't lift weights yet, he rode the exercise bike or jogged around the indoor track.

I went to my room and did my homework, then fell asleep on my bed, waking up around dinnertime. Franklin was talking to my parents in the living room. He seemed happy and relaxed, like the Franklin I used to know.

"Get dressed up," he said. "I'm taking everyone out to eat tonight." So we all went to Friday's and had a good time.

Things were pretty quiet for those few weeks before Christmas. We still worked at Jackson's on weekends, which kept my father busy until the unemployment checks started to come in. And during the week, Franklin tinkered with him around the house. Sometimes Franklin still looked sad, but he seemed to have more energy, like he was on a mission—one he let me be part of on Christmas Eve.

JOHN SMITH AND SONS

December 24 was very cold, with a windchill of about zero. Franklin had told me to set aside the day, that he was going to take me to breakfast and then to get my father's Christmas present. I asked him what it was but he wouldn't tell me. When we left the house, he bypassed our car and started walking down the street.

"Aren't we going to drive?" I asked.

"No. After breakfast we're going to take the bus." He seemed strangely happy.

I shook my head and said, "Well, I hope it's on time."

While we were eating at a local deli, I asked again if the Marines were going to send him back to Iraq.

"I don't want to talk about that today."

"But can they force you to go?"

"But I want to," he said. He was sitting across from me in a booth, fiddling with his scrambled eggs. He wore a light-green crewneck sweater over a white button-down dress shirt, so he looked more like a teacher than a soldier.

"Why would you want to go back there?" I asked.

"Because I don't want to let the other guys down."

"But you were wounded."

He sighed. "It's not that simple. I'm looking at alterna-tives, and things have changed since Dad got laid off. I think I may be able to go back briefly in a noncombat situation, then come home and help out here. I told them about Dad."

"What would you do here?"

He stopped eating and folded his hands in front of his plate. "You aren't going to let this go, are you?"

"Sorry."

"Look, we're buying Dad a new pickup truck. A real beauty. It's red, a few years old, and it has what they call a cargo fiberglass body that fits into it. It can hold all his tools."

"But he's not working."

"But he will be. The only good thing about this reces-sion is that you can get houses real cheap. They're pretty beat up, but you know Dad can fix anything. I often wondered why he never started his own business in the first place. He's always pointing to our coat of arms, talking about those John Smiths who owned property. Now he can have his chance. I've some money saved, and because I'm a Marine, I can get a home loan. I can buy a two- or three-family, Dad can renovate it, and we can either sell or rent it out. That will keep him busy until I get back, and you can help him on weekends."

"So we'll all be working together?"

"Just on weekends. You have to go to college. If you want to work with us after that, fine. But I'm serious about college, you understand?"

I nodded. "Does Dad know anything about this?"

"Nope," he said, smiling. "But Mom does."

After breakfast, we took a bus to a Ford dealership, and Franklin took care of the paperwork while I climbed behind the wheel and watched them attach a sign he'd had a specialty shop make. It read JOHN SMITH AND SONS: HOME RENOVATIONS. After Franklin was done, we drove home. The truck was so large and solid I thought I was inside a tank, but the ride was smooth. About two miles from home, Franklin called my mother. He had told her to bring my father to the picture window when she heard a honk.

We pulled into the driveway, and Franklin beeped the horn, positioning the truck so my father would see the sign on the driver's side door. A minute later he appeared at the window in a white T-shirt, pajama bottoms, with a newspaper in one hand, reading glasses in the other. Franklin and I got out of the truck and stood next to the sign, and Franklin wrapped his arm around my shoulder. In an instant, my father put it together, shaking his head while my mother hugged him.

Later that night, when I took out the garbage, I opened the lid, and there, all wrinkled and balled up on top of a green plastic garbage bag, was my father's shirt and hat from the cleaning company.

"JUST LET IT END, DUDE"

After Franklin found out he didn't have to return to Iraq, after we fixed up Jackson's house, and after Angel seemed to have become a normal human being, Lucky, Jorge, and I were hanging out at my house one rainy April Saturday afternoon, when out of the blue, Jorge asked, "How did Houdini die, anyway?"

"Appendicitis," I said.

"You're kidding, right?"

"No."

"You mean this guy tried to kill himself his whole life and then dies of something as stupid as appendicitis."

Lucky laughed.

"Man, that's nuts."

That day, besides playing video games, Jorge and Lucky were helping me find an ending for my novel. They had read it and had reacted very differently. They both realized Franklin was the real hero of the book, though Lucky thought he was a close second. He already had decided on an actor to play his role, some kid who starred in a basketball movie called *Jumpshot*.

"Thats guy's a wimp," Jorge said.

"But girls dig him," Lucky responded. "All they have to do is dye his hair red."

Jorge liked the action in my book, especially the sections with him telling Angel off, but at first he was angry, saying that if anyone read it and made fun of him, he'd sue me. I said all he'd get was my autographed football, which made him laugh and forget his complaint.

But I still needed an ending to my story, and my mind was a blank.

"I think it should have a happy ending," Lucky said. "We should all become mayors of Providence surrounded by twenty clones of Fiona Rodriguez and we could make Angel chief of police, so he can put a beat-down on anyone we don't like."

"Nah," Jorge said, "Kids like those books where some goofball on a dragon flies out of the sky and saves everyone. I think you should have Da Nang drink some magic potion so that he'll be as big as that Clifford dog, then let him go to Gregory's house and eat him."

I laughed but I reminded them about the last rule for writing a bestselling kid's novel: "Create a happy ending because people won't buy books that say the world is a lousy and confusing place."

"But it is," Jorge said.

Lucky shook his head. "I'd just let it end, dude."

"What do you mean?"

"Let it end wherever it wants to."

"I agree," Jorge said. "The heck with everybody's rules. What do those writers know about kids, anyway? And if people are too dumb to understand our lives, or if we get on their nerves, then all I can say to them is 'Take a hike.'"

Jorge had a point, but he missed something very huge. If you remember, that Mr. Peterson guy said I'd never be the same person if I wrote a book, and I've come to see he was right. Life used to be this big blur of unconnected events. I never understood why people acted weird, and I never thought they could change much.

But being a writer made me look closely at people, maybe even care more about them. I know this sounds weird, but it also made me see a wacky order to things, that maybe Lucky had to get hurt so that Angel could change, and maybe Jackson had to lose an arm so Franklin would join the Marines and get shot and then come back and set my father up in business. None of the "Ten Rules for Writing a Kid's Novel" prepared me for such a cool revelation, but if I ever become a famous writer, I know I'll put it first on my list.

BOOKS JOHN SMITH, JR., AKA HOUDINI, MIGHT HAVE READ

Brandon, Ruth. *The Life and Many Deaths of Harry Houdini*. New York: Random House Trade Paperbacks, 2003.

Carlson, Laurie. *Harry Houdini for Kids: His Life and Adventures with 21 Magic Tricks and Illusions*. Chicago: Chicago Review Press, 2009.

Fleishman, Sid. *Escape!: The Story of the Great Houdini*. New York: Greenwillow Books, 2006.

Kalush, William, and Larry Sloman. *The Secret Life of Harry Houdini: The Making of America's First Superhero*. New York: Atria, 2007.

Lutes, Jason. Illustrated by Nick Bertozzi. *Houdini: The Handcuff King*. New York: Hyperion Books, 2008.

Selznick, Brian. *The Houdini Box*. New York: Atheneum, 2008.

Silverman, Kenneth. *Houdini!!!: The Career of Ehrich Weiss*. New York: Perennial, 1997.

Welsh, CEL. Illustrated by Lalit Singh. *Harry Houdini*
(Campfire Graphic Novels). India: Campfire, 2010.

SOURCES
Brown, Derren, and Harry Houdini. *On Deception*.
London: Hesperus Press, 2009.
Houdini, Harry. *Houdini on Magic*. Mineola, New York:
Dover Publications, 1953.

TURN THE PAGE FOR THE FIRST CHAPTER OF
PETER JOHNSON'S NEXT BOOK:

THE LIFE AND TIMES OF BENNY ALVAREZ

THE GLASS-HALF-FULL-HALF-EMPTY EPISODE

First, a test:

Let's say you're cruising on your skateboard down a street you know better than the secret places where you stash forbidden sticks of gum or that red joy buzzer you trick your younger brother with, when out of nowhere a squirrel cuts you off, making you fall and break your ankle. Bad luck? Punishment for the times you lied to your parents or pranked your older sister? Or is it a sign to be prepared for the unexpected?

And when you're sitting at home watching old reruns of *Tom and Jerry* with your broken ankle resting on a chair while your best friend draws pictures of vampires on your cast, are you mad because your soccer season is as dead as

1

a fly trapped between your front screen and picture window? Or do you look at the bright side and say, "Although my foot hurts worse than getting beat by a girl in arm wrestling, I could've broken my neck"?

"It's about the way you view the world" is what my mother would say, and what she's saying right now for the hundredth time. She's pointing to a half-full glass of water sitting on the kitchen table. The first time she used this expression, I looked up its definition in *Proteus: A Word Dictionary and Thesaurus for Children, with Explanations of Well-Known Phrases*, which me and my friends Beanie and Jocko just call the Book. I even memorized the entry: *The glass half empty or half full is a common expression used to determine the way someone views the world, whether someone is an optimist or a pessimist. That is, whether they see a glass with an even amount of water in it as being half full or half empty.*

I often wonder how long it takes my mother to perfectly measure the water. Does she tape a ruler to the outside of the glass, or follow a scientific formula, like the ones that confuse me on science exams, especially when they try to be funny: "If Beth has a gallon cereal bowl, and it's half filled with milk, will it still be half filled when she adds cereal?"

"Only a cow has a gallon cereal bowl," I complain to Ms. Butterfield, aka Ms. Demigoddess, or Ms. D for

2

short, who's been strong-armed into proctoring my science exam. "Just take the test, Benny."

But it's a trick question. Are we talking about oatmeal, Froot Loops, Cheerios? Are we talking about whole milk, 2 percent, or skim?

"Just take the test, Benny," Ms. D counters again with her excruciatingly pleasant (the Book would say "glorious") smile, a smile you can't say no to. Ms. D could tell you to stick your head in a toilet bowl for two minutes, and you'd gladly do it as long as she kept smiling. But back to the glass-half-full-half-empty episode.

There's something different about the glass today. When my mother asks me whether it's half full or half empty, I usually nudge the table and watch her face cringe as the water vibrates, making her point hard to prove. But this time nothing happens, as if the water's frozen, even though the glass isn't cold when I touch it.

My father, who's also at the table, peers over his morning paper and chuckles, like he's sharing a private joke with my mother. My sister, Irene, who's toying with her scrambled eggs while working on an extra-credit question for AP Biology, says, "Hmmmmmm." And my nine-year-old brother, Crash, angrily blurts out, "It's a dirty trick."

Normally, I pay as much attention to Crash as I do to the yelping of our pug dog, Spot, who's twelve years old, smells like a dead rat no matter how much we groom him, and has half his bottom teeth missing. But this time I say, "What's bugging you today, Crash?"

Crash has flaming-red hair and bright-green eyes the size of bottle caps. His skin's as pale as flour, but when he's mad, his face glows like a ripe tomato, and he's certainly mad now. He points angrily at my mother. "I heard her talking about it. She paid some guy to glue a piece of plastic in the glass. She got it made especially for you." Next, he's pointing at my father. "And *he* said to get it mounted like a trophy and have 'Benny Alvarez: Mr. Negativity' printed on it."

If Irene or I spoke like this to our parents, we'd be in lockdown for a week, but my mother leans over and pats Crash on the head, while my father lowers his newspaper, still amused.

"Don't call your mother 'she,'" he says.

"But it's a dirty trick."

Irene pauses from her extra-credit assignment, addressing Crash in the adult voice she uses when she's trying to act like a school counselor. "Crash," she says, "talk like that keeps you from being a productive human being." So Irene has finally realized Crash is an alien.

Now here's the hard part. Any other guy my age would tell his sister to stop acting superior, or he'd wait until later

4

and mix some toothpaste into her acne cream. I've read all those books where the teenage older sister is nasty and moody and hates her brother, but Irene's the nicest person you'll ever meet. You could tell her a meteor is about to strike, and she'd be more interested in photographing it for posterity than running for cover.

"I'm already a human being," Crash says.

"And a cool one at that," Irene says, "but not very positive."

And there's truth to that. If I'm Mr. Negativity, Crash is the Cantankerous Kid, which is why everyone tiptoes around him, hoping he'll change and not set the house on fire, or maybe they feel bad for naming him Crash after a rich uncle who died on safari a hundred years ago.

But my sister still isn't done. "I think everyone in the family wants you to be happy, Crash, and as Mom says, it's all about attitude." With that, she looks around the table for support. For some reason, I nod (my sister can make you do things like that, like she's a good witch), my father laughs again, and my mother says, "We need to talk about school, Benny."

"School?"

"Yes, school."

My mother volunteers to help at recess, so she sees Ms. D almost every day, and in yesterday's "Benny discussion," my response to the science test came up.

"First, I must stress that Ms. Butterfield said you were not loud or disrespectful, but that your constant questions disrupted the exam."

"It depends on what you mean by 'constant questions.' If you need an answer, there's no limit to the number of questions you should ask."

My father lowers his paper, impressed by my reasoning.

"You're just trying to avoid responsibility for rude behavior, Benny," my mother says.

The Book would have said "weasel out," but I let it slide and go on. "You want me to get As in science, right?"

My father looks interested now, wondering where I'm going with this.

"Of course we do."

"Then how can I get an A if I don't understand the question?"

"He has a point, Margaret," my father says.

"Don't encourage him, Colin."

"I'm with Dad," Crash exclaims, the color of his face back to normal.

"You're all missing Mom's point," Irene interjects.

"Yes," my mother says, holding up the glass. "I had this made, hoping we'll avoid this conversation in the future. I thought you'd place it on your dresser, so it will be the first thing you see in the morning and you'll say, 'I'll go with the glass half full today.'"

Inspired by my mother's speech, Irene nods her head so vigorously, she almost falls off her chair.

Crash mumbles, "Fat chance."

And my father, trying to save face with my mother, says, "You never know, Benny," though he doesn't look too convinced.

"But first," my mother continues, "I need to know that you understand the symbolism of the glass."

"Come on, Mom," I say.

"So I don't have to repeat it?"

"Trust me, I get it."

So I take the glass upstairs and place it on my dresser. Why? First, because I made my point. Second, because I don't want to be late for school. And third, because I love my mother, and if she wants me to wake up every morning staring at this strange trophy, I'll do it, though I know I'll always see the glass as half empty. Irene, my mom, Ms. D, and I'm sure my archenemy, Claudine, would think that makes me negative, but that depends on how you define negativity.

THE BOOK

I was about seven when my mother first feared I was becoming "negative." It all started one morning after my father delivered one of his many rants on politics. My mother asked him to tone it down, saying the world wasn't going to end soon and that it was best to focus on all the good things people do. More important, she added, she was beginning to notice the same kind of attitude in me, as if she thought negativity was contagious, or passed down genetically, like blond hair and blue eyes.

"Negative?" my father protested. "I call it enthusiasm for my beliefs. Instead of plopping down in front of the TV, Margaret, I read and develop opinions. The rich are getting richer and want the rest of us to be their gardeners, and people might be more inclined to end these stupid wars if their own kids were soldiers. I don't like thinking about these things, but you can't just paste smiley faces on the refrigerator"—my mother does this—"or . . ." And as my father rampaged on, my mother looked at Irene, who was eleven at the time, both of them nodding knowingly at me and my father, as if to say "Case closed."

Later the word "negative" followed me around like a bad stink, and when a word seems tattooed on your forehead, when teachers, people you hardly know, call you something, it's time to examine the word.

Word Warriors to the rescue.

The Word Warriors are me and my best friends, Jocko and Beanie. Those aren't their real names, but they decided you needed a nickname to join our club. I don't blame them. Jocko's real name is Reginald and Beanie's is Jefferson. Beanie didn't like his name because he said no one trusts a kid with a last name for a first name, especially if he's black, and Jocko said he always wanted to be called Jocko after some WWF wrestler who died years ago in a car accident.

I told them I didn't want a nickname. I'm president of the club, so what could they say? I actually like my name, even though it doesn't fit. When people meet me, they expect me to speak Spanish because of the "Alvarez," but in fact, no one in my family looks Hispanic or speaks Spanish or has even been to Spain or South America or Mexico. I guess my father had a great-great-great-great-grandfather named Alvarez who married an Irishwoman. After that it was Irish plus Irish until my father married my mother, who's French. So if you're expecting a rush of Spanish when I get worked up, you're going to be disappointed.

Which brings me to the Book.

As I said, the Book is *Proteus: A Word Dictionary and Thesaurus for Children, with Explanations of Well-Known Phrases* by A. J. Logos. I came across it when Borders closed and they were having a huge book sale. At first, I refused to go with my father because he was bent on protesting the closing, wanting to give a tough time to "the buzzards feeding off the death of a beautiful animal." But I decided to give him moral support, and even he ended up buying a book on golf for my grandfather, though not until he had complained out loud for ten minutes to anyone who'd listen about "greedy corporations."

While he patrolled the store, I scanned the kids' section, coming across a pile of little blue books with gold emblems on the covers. Small enough to fit in your back pocket, they were stacked alongside hundreds of those stupid vampire novels Jocko reads. The dictionary part didn't blow me away, but when I paged through the thesaurus, I got excited. I guess I had always known about the thesaurus, but I had never held one in my hand. The first word I looked up was "dumb." I found "inarticulate, mute, silent, dim-witted, moronic, thick, dense," and the list went on. That's when I realized a thesaurus could actually be fun. For example, there's this one bully in school named Big Joe, and sometimes it's hard to tell whether he's a jerk or plain dumb, but I know if I call him dumb, he'll have three of his friends hold me down while he kicks soccer balls into my face. But I might be able to get away with "thick" or "dense," and if I call him "inarticulate," he'll think I'm complimenting him.

Now my mother would say I had discovered ammunition to aid me in my so-called negative approach to life, but, if you look at a thesaurus, even "negative" isn't the right word. Consider some of its synonyms: "adverse, antagonistic, contrary, dissenting, repugnant." You could see me as contrary or adverse, but that's not necessarily a bad thing. The Founding Fathers were contrary, and if they hadn't been, we'd all be talking funny and wearing bowler hats. And no one can ever accuse me of being repugnant. I wouldn't even like to be called antagonistic, but sometimes you have to be if you want to change something, and there's always something to change at school, especially with Claudine infecting the hallways with her nonsense.

Maybe none of this excites you, but Jocko and Beanie, after I gave them *Proteus*, could see the interesting possibilities of playing with words. Beanie nailed it after Jocko said one afternoon that he was "scared" of that week's English exam. Trying to cheer Jocko up, Beanie opened the Book and read, "'Scared: alarmed, dismayed, worried, terrified, paralyzed, upset.' No, Jocko, you aren't 'scared' of your exam. You're alarmed and worried and upset. You're scared of spiders, and terrified of your father, and paralyzed when you have to talk in front of class."

"Bravo!" I said.

"Thanks," Jocko said, "though I still feel scared."

In his own way, Jocko was right, but he still saw the logic of Beanie's comment, and he was the one who suggested we start a club. "Besides the thesaurus," he said, "let's use a new word or expression from the Book every day, but it's got to be a weird one, something the other two will have to guess at, and you can never know it's coming."

Beanie and I liked this idea. Then we all agreed to be what you might call an "exclusive" club, meaning we'd have only three members. If that sounds bad, then think of us as being "particular" or "classy," or if you want to be nasty, I guess we'll have to live with "narrow-minded" or "snobbish."

EVERYONE THINKS BENNY ALVAREZ IS
MR. NEGATIVITY. ACCORDING TO BENNY,
HE JUST SEES THINGS AS THEY ARE.

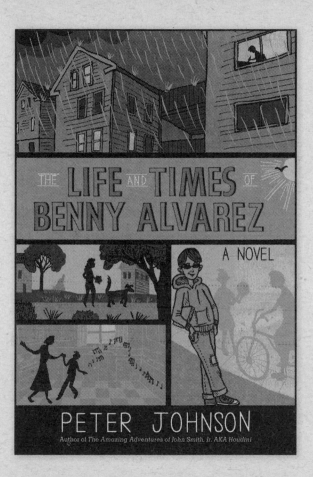

Half-full, half-empty . . . What's the difference?

HARPER
An Imprint of HarperCollinsPublishers

www.harpercollinschildrens.com